One Night

A novel by

E. A. DeBoest

One Night

This book is a work of fiction. Names, characters, places, and incidents either are products of the author's imagination or are used fictitiously. Any resemblance to actual events or locals or persons, living or dead, is entirely coincidental.

ISBN - 13: 978-1722893392
ISBN - 10: 1722893397
Copyright 2018 by Elizabeth A. DeBoest

Manufactured in the United States of America

Books by E. A. DeBoest

<u>Construction of the Heart Series</u>
3 Erotic Romance Novels
Construction of the Heart Vol 1
Sealing of the Heart Vol 2
Expansion of the Heart Vol 3

One Night

One Night

Chapter One

The wind whistles through the streets of Chicago, causing the tree branches to sway and the leaves to rustle. The sky is a grayish-blue color with dark, gloomy clouds stretching as far as the eyes can see, and fat raindrops plummet to the ground. It's not how I envisioned this evening playing out, but maybe it will bring more people into the bar.

I sigh as I look out my apartment window. I've always loved the rain. I find the sounds of raindrops soothing and the sounds of a thunderstorm exciting. And sometimes I enjoy the rain washing over me, even drenching me. But tonight is my debut night. I just want it to be perfect. I sigh again. I guess I should look at it as a sign, a sign because rain has always been my friend. So maybe it will bring me good luck.

But I still need to calm my nerves, not nerves from the weather, but nerves because I'm elated and anxious at the same time. This is the biggest night of my life. It will either make me or break me. So I grab a shot glass out of my kitchen cupboard and the bottle of whiskey out of my fridge. A little alcohol should help.

The brown liquor runs down my throat and instantly warms my insides. So I take another shot and relax just a bit more.

But I know what will automatically calm me down and loosen me up, plus it will help get me better in the mood to recite my work to a bunch of strangers. So I retreat to my bedroom and strip all my clothes off.

I need an orgasm. I need to masturbate.

One Night

I take my box of toys out of my closet and bring it to my bed. I pull back my blue-green comforter and climb on top of my white cotton sheets. Then I open the box and search for just the right toy.

I love sex toys. They are essential for being properly single in today's world. An occasional warm, male body is always nice, but I'm not really down for one-night stands, and fuck buddies with no strings attached are hard to find.

But I do have a sex friend, and I keep him at arm's length. The problem is that he has strings and seems to be somewhat attached to me. He knows where I stand, but I still don't let him get too close. You see, I want spontaneity, a wild romance and explosive fireworks, and hot, untamed passion in my life, and I won't settle for anything less. So my fuck friend is kept on a long leash. But hopefully, the right man will come along and light me up from the inside out and I can let my buddy loose once and for all.

I grab not one toy but two, my butt plug and my string of silver pearls. I'm feeling kind of naughty, maybe it's the whiskey, but I need to feel full and come hard. But first things first, I need to make my pussy wet.

I have a full-length, stand-up mirror in my room that is positioned in an ideal spot, kitty corner, and it allows me to see my whole reflection directly from my bed. I love watching myself masturbate. It's always so intense like this, so I always do it this way.

I pull my long, thick, chestnut locks into a ponytail, and then I spread my bended legs wide open, giving me a great view of my freshly waxed sex. I lean back just a bit into my pillows and stare at my sexy reflection. I bite my bottom lip, and then I place my hands on my breasts and squeeze them into my fists repeatedly. My nipples get hard, it feels so good.

I can't conceal my self-indulgence, and I let out my vocal satisfaction, moaning my gratification.

My breasts overflow in my hands. How I long for the day when the man of my dreams takes my fully round, plump breasts in his big, strong hands and makes me come just from his touch. Damn, the thought makes me moan louder.

I pull on my nipples as I gaze at my highly aroused self. God, I look so hot, so pornographic. I should video record myself one of these days. This is too good to not watch over and over again.

The heat is rising between my thighs, and I can feel the moisture building inside my pussy. I'm so ready to kick my pleasure up another notch. I bite my bottom lip, pull on my nipples harder, and grind my sex and my ass into the mattress, not being able to resist the deep need taking over me.

I love assaulting my breasts and my nipples. And I love pushing my fingers inside myself, two fingers usually, and sometimes I push two fingers from one hand and two fingers from my other hand inside me at the same time. It fills me when I don't have the desire to use dildos or vibrators, and it always makes me come hard.

But tonight, I'm just going to stick a single finger in me, just to measure how wet I am. And if I'm honest, I'm craving a little taste, too. And I have to admit, I taste really good.

I glide my fingers from both hands slowly down my body until I reach my folds. I open up my smooth pussy lips, exposing my clit, and then dip my finger inside. I moan. I'm nice and wet. I circle my finger around my walls and move it in and out a couple times. Then I pull it out and begin spreading my sticky wetness all through my folds and all around my back hole. I also coat the butt plug in my fluids. I don't need any lube.

I bring my sticky finger to my mouth and wrap my lips around it. I suck it hard, cleaning it and enjoying my taste. Then I lick my lips and wink at myself in the mirror.

My core and my backside are both equally craving to be penetrated. I'm so ready to be filled.

I pick up my string of silver pearls and insert them in my warm, wet mouth. They need to be lubricated, so my tongue moves them around. Then I pull them out. They're glistening. I grin mischievously at myself.

My body temperature has risen, and my heart rate has accelerated in anticipation. I am so turned on.

I stuff the silver pearls inside my hungry pussy and moan loudly. I push the butt plug inside my just as hungry ass and moan even louder. I adjust to the invasion, allowing it to claim me as I sink a little more into the mattress and get a little more comfortable against my pillows. Then I pause for a second. This view is so incredibly hot.

My thoughts, not just my vision, are consumed by the kink. Oh fuck, I'm finally full. And goddamn, it feels so fucking good.

I start moving the butt plug by twisting it back and forth inside me. I quietly moan yet continuously.

The rain gets louder and louder as it aggressively smacks against my window, and then I hear the first booms of a thunderstorm. Now this is even more exciting, and the sounds of the storm rouse me to be fiercer in my actions. And that intensifies my pleasure everywhere.

I palm my sex, causing some of my sticky wetness to drip onto my hand. I rub my fluids on my clit, and then I begin rubbing my clit, circling it with two fingers. And as I'm doing that, I begin moving the butt plug in and out and still twisting it as I do. It's all very fierce.

I bite my bottom lip as I stare at the porn playing in my mirror, and my moans get louder, and my breathing turns into panting.

God, this is precisely what I need. It's sad that no man has ever been able to give me mind-blowing orgasms, or any ecstasy for that matter. Don't get me wrong, I have orgasms with men, just not the over-the-top intense ones that I'm able to give myself. So far, I'm my best lay. God, I hope that changes soon.

My clit is swollen and hard. My inner walls are swelling around the pearls. And I'm pushing the butt plug in me at a quicker pace. My body is building and building to a powerful release. I just wonder if my neighbors can hear me through the walls. But fuck it if they do, this is too good to try to keep my noises down.

I take my fingers off my clit and move my hand back up to my breast, where I squeeze it into my fist, and then I start tugging on my nipple over and over, and rather roughly. Rough not painful, just the way I like it.

But my other breast wants some more action, too. So I push the butt plug inside me again and leave it filling me, and then I move my hand up to my lonely breast. I squeeze it into my fist, and then I start tugging on my nipple over and over roughly. My twins have equal attention now, and I'm getting so close to exploding.

I'm moaning so loud, and I'm panting so hard, that I can't hear the storm anymore. I'm completely lost in my reflection. I'm definitely recording myself next time.

My pleasure is in charge, and it has a mind of its own. I absentmindedly begin grinding my ass and my sex into the mattress. And Jesus, the pressure feels so fucking good.

My grinding motions are pushing the butt plug firmly in my backside, and it's also making the pearls swirl around vigorously in my wet warmth. And I'm so full, and it feels so good, that I grind faster and harder.

"Shit," I voice as I pinch and tug my nipples. I'm right there, so close, my orgasm is approaching.

My entire body begins convulsing, and then my orgasm spills out of me. It starts dripping onto my sheets, and then I pull the pearls out of me and press my thumb to my clit. I come even harder and feel my fluids saturating the sheets more, making a big puddle all around my sex and my backside.

After a few minutes, I somewhat start to catch my breath, but I'm not done. I want more.

I stuff the pearls in my mouth, throw my head back into the pillows, and I decide to put two fingers inside me and move the butt plug some more. So I move two fingers in and out of my pussy at the same time that I push and pull the butt plug in and out of my ass. And I reach ecstasy again. I come hard all over again.

I slam the butt plug into me, and then pull the string of pearls out of my mouth. I scream out my pleasures as my body convulses once again and spills out more fluids. I'm lost in a hazy reflection.

"Fuck, fuck, fuck," I murmur, and lay unmoving in my bed. That was amazing. I'm spent, so exhausted, finally feeling extremely relaxed, and better yet, I'm sated.

I remove my fingers and the butt plug. I stretch out my legs and melt into the mattress. Then I reach for my phone on my nightstand. I set the alarm on it. Thirty minutes should suffice. I could use a nap after fucking myself so thoroughly. So I set my phone down next to me, pull my comforter over me, and I close my drooping eyelids. Then I yawn and let the sleep take me.

Chapter Two

"You're going to be great. The crowd is going to love every word," Abby tells me. She's my very best friend. She always has been for as far back as I can remember. We grew up together.

"Thanks," I say as I sit on a barstool next to her. I'm at a hotspot bar in the heart of Chicago, and I'm ready to present my work to the awaiting audience.

The bar is called Intoxication. It's a big place, and the coolest people always frequent it, sometimes celebrities stop by as well. It's the perfect place to present my writings. That's right, I'm a writer. I write romantic and erotic poems, an occasional short story, and I'm trying my hand at writing my first full-length novel. So naturally, I was thrilled when the owner wanted to add me to the entertainment and asked me to recite my poems one night a week.

This bar has live entertainment every night, usually the finest locals that are on their way to becoming stars. Live bands play here all the time, plus solo singers and rappers and poets. It's probably the coolest bar in Chicago, probably the coolest bar in all of Illinois for that matter, and I'm beyond excited to be a part of it.

"Here," Abby says, handing me a shot of whiskey. I take it and swallow it all in one gulp. "Have fun," she says, smiling.

"Oh, I will." I smile back. After my intense, mind-blowing orgasms not too long ago, I'm feeling great, confident, and sexy.

I'm wearing skinny jeans that are nice and tight in all the right places, a red belly shirt, and matching red high heels. My lips are coated in red lipstick. I've applied the right amount of eyeliner, eye shadow, and mascara to my eyelids and lashes, giving me the smoky eye look. My hair has waves in it, and it's hanging down my back. I think I fit the part flawlessly for what I'm about to do.

The MC gets on stage and grabs the Mic. "Ladies and gentlemen," he begins, "can I have your attention, please?" He waits for the crowd to quiet down. Then he continues, "Tonight your ears are going to be filled with the seductive words from the lovely and sexy, Miss Savannah Lewis." There are a few whistles and cat-calls from the crowd. "Please put your hands together for the erotic poetess," the MC finishes.

The crowd erupts into an energetic applause with some whistling, and that's my cue. I rise off the barstool and saunter onto the stage with a sexy strut in my step and my head held high. I've been looking forward to this night for a while now, and I'm so, so ready.

I take the Mic in my hand, having perfect posture, and look out into the crowd. There are a ton of people here tonight, and I'm thrilled. The applause dies down, the crowd gets quiet, and all eyes are on me. This is it.

"Hi," I say in a sultry voice. "How are you all doing tonight?" The crowd hoots, hollers, and cheers in response. I smile and continue, "This stage has had some of the coolest and hippest artists gracing it with their talents, and I'm so honored to be included." There are more hoots, hollers, and cheers, all in agreement with me. "I'm a writer of the romantic, erotic genre, and tonight I'm going to share some of my literary finesse with you." The audience is energetic and animated with their approval, clapping, whistling, and cheering. It makes me feel very welcome, and I instantly feel like I belong here. I've found my professional home.

I keep my voice in an extremely sultry tone, channeling all my sexy swag, and speaking my seductive and hot words slowly, and emphasizing just the right ones when needed, and I begin, "This is called, Desire."

There are several whistles from the crowd, and all eyes continue to drink in my presence.

"Desire
His vehement eyes are watching me

So raw and so ferociously untamed
Desire
As he stalks toward me
I see that he's hungry, he's wild, he's barely contained
Desire
He steals me
Taking my yearning body
And making me scream his name
Desire
He whispers in my ear
And his breath washes over me
Sending shivers down my spine
Desire
He grabs me
And pulls me closer
Locking me in his arms, firmly entwined
Desire
His voice is deep, authoritative, and powerful
As he commands me
In his masterful way
But what did he whisper in my ear?
His needs, his wants, his desires
For me and only me
He said, "I'm going to make you mine."
Desire"

I finish, and everyone in attendance erupts into rambunctious applause, with some people even giving me a standing ovation, plus loud whistling all around. It's amazing, and I did it. I smile into the crowd, and then I blow them a kiss and wave.

"Thank you," I say into the Mic, and then exit the stage. I take a seat back at the bar and next to my friend, who's got a big smile spread across her face.

"You were great!" Abby beams. "A complete natural," she adds.

"Thanks," I say with a smile.

A band, Bass and Beauty, takes the stage next and play a collection of their best songs. And they're really good, quite catchy.

"I felt so good being up there."

"I could tell," Abby says. "You looked so confident and so sexy, plus you sounded so incredibly sexy."

"Good. That's exactly what I tried to give the crowd."

"Oh, you did," she says, and her eyes smile at me. "They were all on the edge of their seats eating up every word, every syllable."

"Perfect, then they will really enjoy the poem that I leave them with a little later tonight."

"You're giving them another one tonight?" she asks, looking at me with quizzical brown eyes.

"Yes," I say, nodding. "Something much more suggestive," I add, and then wink at her.

"Very cool," she says. "Then we should have more drinks."

"Sounds good," I say, smiling.

"I ordered us some food, too. Chicken tenders and fries," she says.

"Great. Thanks."

Just then, my parents approach us at the bar, and they're both smiling proudly. My parents are great. They're laid-back, carefree, and fun, just like me. And they support my writing career completely.

"Savannah, darling, you are brilliant," my mom gushes. I stand up, and we give each other a hug.

"Thank you," I murmur as I'm held in her embrace. She kisses my cheek and releases me.

"You're really good, Sweetie, really good," my dad gushes as well. We hug each other, too.

"Thanks, Dad," I murmur, and then he releases me.

"Seeing you on the stage filled my heart with so much joy," my mom says. "I am so proud of you."

"I agree, Sweetheart," my dad says to my mom, and kisses her on the cheek, and then he takes her hand and laces his fingers through hers.

My parents are very affectionate and love one another immensely. They're always all over each other, and in public, too. I find it very inspiring, and that's where I get my ideas on romance and love from, from watching them. They've been great role models. I hope to have an obsession of my own to love someday soon.

"Let's dance, Beautiful," my dad says to my mom.

"Yes, let's," she agrees.

"Have fun you two," I say, smiling. "I'm speaking one more poem before the night is over," I inform them.

"Oh good," my mom says, smiling.

"We look forward to it, Sweetie," my dad says, and then he takes my mom onto the dance floor.

"Your parents are so hot," Abby says.

"Yeah, they really are," I agree.

"They arrived here right as you were walking on stage. They were all over each other, but paused for a minute to say hello to me, and then they sat down and were very touchy-feely as you were speaking your sensual words."

"That sounds exactly like my parents." We both laugh.

My parents definitely know how to turn anything steamy. That's just how hot they are, hot for each other, hot to watch, and they're hot in the looks department as well. For being in their fifties, they are healthy and fit, energetic and always on the go, and I'm happy to admit that I look a lot like my mom, and a bit like my dad at times, too. Hot genes, hot personalities, and lots of hotness all around, that's the Lewis family.

And then another hottie from the Lewis family approaches me, my sister, Lacy. She's my older sister by a couple of years. She's newly single and welcoming it with open arms. She's the manager at my parents' store, an erotic store that sells sex toys, lingerie, and very steamy books. It's called Ooh, Erotic Pleasures. I help out there a lot, and I sometimes write while I'm there. And my parents are going to sell my writings there, too, as soon as I get them all published.

"Hey, Little Vixen," Lacy says, smiling at me.

"Hi," I say, smiling, and we give each other a hug.

"Hi, Abby," my sister says after she lets me go.

"Hi, Lacy," Abby says, smiling, and they hug as well.

"Did you just get here?" I ask my sister.

"No," she says, shaking her head. "I walked in when you were being introduced."

"And, what did you think?"

"You're hot," she adamantly states. "Your look, your voice, your words, you're hot." She winks at me. "And I loved it," she adds.

"Thank you." I smile.

"Mom and Dad seem to be having a good time."

"Yeah, they really are," I agree as I glance at them on the dance floor. There's a little bumping and grinding action between them, and it's not really a surprise.

"Are you staying?" Abby asks my sister. "Cause Savannah's going on stage again a little later."

"I'm most definitely staying." She smiles. "I wouldn't miss my little sister's big night, plus I brought a couple of friends. We plan on partying, maybe flirt with some hot guys."

"Well, there are plenty of hot guys here tonight," Abby says.

"I know. My eyes have been roaming all over from the moment I sat down." All three of us laugh. Lacy is aggressive and blunt, and she's a total man-eater when she's single. She's been known to have a few one-night stands. We may look a lot alike, but the way we deal with men is where we differ. "Alright, I'm going to get back to my friends," she says, and kisses my cheek. "I know you're going to make this entire bar of people love you as you make them extremely hot and bothered with more of your words."

"That's the plan." I wink at her. Then she walks back to where her friends are sitting, and there are already a couple of guys at their table.

"Here," Abby says, handing me shot of whiskey.

"Liquor before beer," I say, and wink at her.

"And we're in the clear," she says, and winks back at me. We both smile at the saying, and then we swallow our shots.

"Your food is almost ready, ladies," the bartender says, smiling and showcasing his dimples. He's cute. He's got an innocent quality to his features, but I bet that's far from the case.

"Great, thanks." Abby smiles at him. They hold each other's gaze for a minute, and then he gets back to work, taking people's drink orders.

"He's cute," I mention.

"He is," she says, and her cheeks get pink.

"You like him," I tease.

"I don't know what you're talking about."

I laugh. "You can't fool me, Abby. You're getting a little flustered just talking about him."

She looks at me like I haven't got a clue as to what I'm saying.

"Don't look at me like that," I tell her. "You're blushing, you like him."

"Maybe," she murmurs.

"Well, I think he likes you. He keeps stealing glances at you."

"What?" she exclaims, and her cheeks turn red now. Then she looks at him, and their eyes meet again, and they lock for a heated moment.

"I see the connection, girl, and I feel it."

"Okay," she says, turning her head toward me. "I like him. I've talked to him a little, and he seems genuinely nice."

"And he's cute," I reiterate.

"Yeah, he's really cute." She smiles, and her blush stays right where it is.

Just then, a young woman approaches me. "Hi," she says. "I hope I'm not disturbing you, but I'm a big fan."

"Hi." I smile. "What's your name?"

"Tammy," she says, smiling.

"It's nice to meet you, Tammy," I say, extending my hand to her. She takes it, and we shake.

"I follow you all over social media, and I'm so excited for your upcoming novel," she says.

"Thank you for your support. I'm excited about my novel, too."

"I hope this isn't too weird, but I printed your latest news letter that you sent out. It happens to have a short story included in it that I instantly fell in love with, and I was hoping you could sign it for me?"

Even though I'm not a published author yet, I have a fairly big following already. I'm on Twitter, Facebook, Instagram, and I have a blog post on Tumblr, plus I send out a news letter to my fans about once a month, sometimes every other month, and every once in a while, I meet someone who loves my work. It's really cool, and it makes all my hard work worth it.

"I'd love to sign it for you," I reply.

"Oh cool, thank you," she says excitedly, and then she pulls the news letter out of her large purse. I take it and sign it and include a little message of encouragement.

"Are you having a good time tonight?" I ask her as I hand her back the news letter.

"Yes, I'm having a great time." She beams.

"I'm glad. I hope you plan on sticking around, because I'm going back on stage later on."

"Oh yeah, I'm staying." She nods.

"Cool."

"Can I just ask you one more thing?"

"Sure."

"Can I get a picture with you?"

"Of course," I say, and stand up.

Tammy takes her phone out of her purse.

"I'll snap the pic," Abby offers.

"Thanks," Tammy says, and gives Abby her phone.

Tammy stands next to me, and Abby takes a picture of us both smiling. Then Abby hands Tammy back her phone.

"Thank you so much," Tammy says.

"You're very welcome," I tell her. "Enjoy the rest of the night." And then she leaves, disappearing into the large crowd.

"That was really cool," Abby says.

"Yeah, that just made my night." I sit back down.

"Your food and beer, ladies," the bartender says, setting chicken fingers, fries, and two Heinekens in front of us.

I'm going to keep quiet and let Abby do the talking. After all, this man is interested in her and her alone.

"Thank you," Abby says meekly as she stares into his eyes.

"You're welcome," he says, and then he winks at her right before he goes back to making drinks.

"If he doesn't ask you out before the end of the night, then something is seriously wrong with him."

"Maybe he's shy," she says.

"Then you should ask him out."

"Maybe I'm too shy."

"Bullshit," I state. "But if you want to play that game, then I'll ask him out for you."

"You wouldn't," she says, her brown eyes getting big in their sockets.

"You know I would."

"Fine," she says. "I'll see how it plays out for the rest of the evening, and then go from there."

"Good."

Abby and I have a lot in common, but when it comes to men, I'm a little more outgoing than her.

"I want to touch his dimples," she admits.

"You think he's got dimples on his ass, too?"

"You're terrible," she says.

"Whatever, I'm sure the thought crossed your mind, too."

She laughs, and so do I. My mind is dirtier and kinkier than hers, but she's not innocent.

We eat our food and drink our beer listening to the band play and talking in-between bites and swigs. And I notice the bartender, whose name I think is Steve and Abby continuing to glance at each other periodically. I'm rooting for them.

The night moves along quickly, and before I know it, it's time for me to take the stage once again.

The MC takes the Mic. "Alright, ladies and gentlemen, it's time to fill your ears with the sexy poetess' words one more time this evening," he announces. The crowd goes wild, whistling, hollering, and cheering louder than they were earlier. I'm hoping it's because they're excited to hear me speak again, but it's probably a combination of that and the alcohol. "Please welcome back to the stage, Miss Savannah Lewis."

The crowd continues with their loud and energetic uproar, as well as their echoing applause. And I rise and walk to the stage with the same sexy strut in my step. I'm ready to give them something that will be hard to forget.

With the Mic in my hand and the crowd calming down, I begin, "I'm going to give you a very erotic poem, something that's naughtier than my previous one." The crowd whistles with excitement. "My words are guaranteed to put a visual in your head that will play out like a porno." The crowd goes wild again, hooting, hollering, and cheering.

I wait for them to get quiet, and all eyes are on me, ready for me to speak my seductive and hot words.

"This is called, Lover's Delight," I say, my voice sultry. I speak my words slowly and emphasizing all the right ones when needed.

This is going to grab their attention, and hopefully, make them remember my name.

"Lover's Delight
He slams me against the wall
And rips my clothes from my craving body
He crushes my lips
He grips my hips
And he pushes his hardness inside me
He's taking me
He's claiming me
And I'm his
Loving his delight
As he takes my body higher
With every delicious stroke
Penetrating me deep
As I pant and moan
And I melt all around him
My body bowing and exploding
With the cream
As it shoots and pours out of me
My cream
It's thick and white
My cream
Coating his cock
My cream
Then his cream
Lover's Delight"

The audience gets really loud, jumping to their feet, clapping, cheering, whistling, hooting, and hollering. And this is by far the loudest they've been all night. It's wonderful, and it's all for me.

"Thank you," I tell the crowd, and I smile brightly. Then I blow them a kiss and wave as I leave the stage.

I walk back to the bar, and Abby is in a deep conversation with the cute bartender. He's leaning into the bar and staring into her eyes as they exchange words. Neither one of them look shy but very comfortable. My rooting for them seems to be paying off.

I don't want to disturb the love connection that's brewing, so I turn on my heel and begin merging into the crowd, ready to do a little mingling before I leave for the evening. But a familiar voice stops me before I get lost in the mass of people.

"Savannah!" Chris shouts. I turn around and amble toward him. He's smiling and looking very yummy, wearing jeans and a blue and white striped buttoned shirt. He's always been nice eye candy. I guess that's why I keep him handy.

Chris is my fuck friend. I met him at a local coffee shop several months ago. He was ahead of me in line and paid for my coffee, and we started talking from there. But I quickly realized that we wouldn't be anything more than friends. I just don't have a romantic spark with him, but he's so good looking that I still wanted to have sex with him, because sometimes a girl needs a hard man to penetrate her. So I gave him my terms, and he accepted, and enthusiastically I might add.

But since he has strings and a bit of an attachment to me, I try to only see him once every few weeks, sometimes even letting a whole month pass by before I see him. He's very respectful and doesn't bother pressing the issue of seeing me more, but I can see it in his eyes that he wishes I would give him more, more time, more of me. But I just can't.

The man that I let into my life fully and give myself to completely will be the one that ignites a flame inside me that can't be extinguished. But Chris is looking good tonight, and after my masturbation session earlier, I'm sort of craving some hard dick to fill my pussy. The question is his place or mine?

"Hi, Chris," I say with a smile.

"You were great," he exclaims.

"Thanks. Did you catch both poems?"

"I did. They were both really hot." He leans in closer and lowers his head, so that his mouth is close to my ear. "You made my dick so hard," he whispers.

"Well then, you're in luck. I need something hard."

"Really," he says, looking excited, but also slightly skeptical, and I don't blame him. I never promised him any sex this evening.

I was just with Chris last weekend, but fuck it. He looks good, and I'm horny. "Yes." I nod. "But I just need to finish up here first with a little socializing and networking."

"You do your thing, Savannah. I'll be at the bar," he says, and then kisses me on the cheek.

Chris heads to the bar and takes a seat, and I merge myself back into the crowd. I talk with several people, new fans and the following that I already have, and it's nice to put faces with my fans. I also talk with my sister and her friends, and then my parents. I'm given lots of compliments and praise from everyone that I've met and talked to tonight. It's really great.

I feel so fucking fantastic, and I'm about to get a good, hard fuck to top it all off.

"Hey," I say to Abby as I approach her at the bar. "How did it go with the cute bartender?" The bartender is at the opposite end of the bar, talking to Chris.

"Great." She smiles. "Steve is taking me out tomorrow night."

"Sweet," I reply. "Well, I'm out of here." I grab my umbrella.

"Are you leaving with Chris?"

"Yeah," I say, nodding.

"You're going to end up breaking that man's heart."

"No. He knows my rules."

"That doesn't matter. Sex is involved, and sex usually always leads to connections and attachments. And I've seen the way he looks at you."

I sigh. I know she's right. "Shit," I murmur. "I guess I should think of something."

"Yeah," she agrees.

"Okay, I will, but after one more hard fuck."

"You're terrible," she says, rolling her eyes.

"I know. You're always reminding me."

"Well, it's true." She shrugs, but she's smiling, so I know she's laughing on the inside.

"See you later, girl." I give her a quick hug.

"Bye. Have fun."

I walk to the other end of the bar and tap Chris on his shoulder. "I'm ready," I murmur close to his ear.

"So am I," he says, finishing his beer and leaving a tip on the bar. He rises off the stool, and we begin walking toward the doors.

I notice it's pouring down rain again. It's been raining for hours. The storm quieted down a lot, and the rain lightened up some when I arrived at the bar this evening, but now it's back to the stormy, big, fat raindrops again. Damn. I don't want to walk home in this, even with my umbrella. I'm five blocks away, but Chris's place is much closer, only two blocks away. We can run there and hopefully not get too wet. So I guess it's his place tonight.

"My place is closer," Chris says, looking at the rain through the doors.

"I was thinking the same thing."

"You want to make a run for it?" he asks me, turning his head toward me and looking at me.

"Yeah, let's go."

Chris opens the door, and I step out, opening my umbrella as I do, and he's right behind me, and then at my side. He takes my hand in his, and I'm instantly made aware again that there's no powerful reaction from me when he touches me. It's exactly why I need to end things between us. I can't continue to tease him and string him along. So after tonight, I'm done.

We start running down the street, and even though I would normally remove my hand from his, I don't, because I could use the support as I run in the rain with my high heels on. I try to shield us both with my umbrella, but it's not really big enough, and we are getting wet, very wet. So we run just a little bit faster.

It only takes a few minutes to get to his apartment, and we are completely soaked when we arrive. So we automatically begin stripping our wet clothes off. Then Chris grabs two towels from his small linen closet and hands me one. I start drying my hair and body, and he wraps his towel around his waist and picks up all of our clothes. He hangs them up, and then he points a fan at them and turns it on. Good boy, he knows I'm not staying the night.

I drop my towel on his bedroom floor, and then I pull back his navy blue comforter and climb onto his bed. I sit at the edge, bend my legs in front of me, and spread them wide. "Make this pussy wet, Chris," I tell him, as he's standing in the doorway of his bedroom, his hard cock visibly present through his towel as he stares at me.

He probably has the same hard-on that he's had all evening at the bar from listening to me speak. Although, I'm sure it's even harder now than it was at the bar, because now I'm naked on his bed and inviting him in for a taste.

"I'd love to," he says, and walks toward me, dropping his towel on floor along the way.

He kneels down in front of me and grips my thighs. Then he lowers his face and starts licking through my slit. I place my hands palms down on the bed on either side of my legs, and I watch him. I love watching, whether it's my reflection in my mirror, or a man giving me the pleasure. I just love watching.

"Ooh, that feels good," I murmur, and I fist the sheets slightly.

He licks through my slit, and sucks on my lips, and sucks on my clit. And he's turning me on. I'm wet and ready for him to push his cock inside me.

"Fuck me, Chris," I tell him. He lifts his head up and looks me in the eyes. "Fuck me," I repeat.

"Goddamn, Savannah, you're so hot," he says as he stands up and walks to his nightstand. He opens it and grabs a condom.

I get off the bed and bend over it instead with my feet firmly on the ground. I want it from the back. I spread my legs wide for him and look over my shoulder at him. He's ripping the condom wrapper open and walking back to me.

"Fuck me hard, Chris," I say, making eye contact with him.

"Shit, Savannah," he says, sheathing his hard cock. "I'm so fucking hard for you."

"Good. Now give it to me."

He pushes his cock inside my sex, and then grips my hips and begins moving in and out. He feels good, and he's a pretty decent lay, but like I said, I'm my best lay to date so far. So if I want to come with Chris inside me, then I'm going to have to help the process.

I move my hand to my clit and start rubbing on it with two fingers as he continues pushing his cock in and out, fast and hard. It swells up fairly quickly, but I want to feel more presser. I want to come as hard as I can.

"Push your thumb in my ass, Chris," I tell him.

"Oh, Savannah," he moans, gripping my hips harder.

"Do it," I command. And he does, pushing his thumb all the way into my ass, and then moving it in and out in rhythm to the movements of his cock.

"Oh fuck," he voices.

"Yes," I cry out in pleasure as I still rub on my clit.

"God, Savannah, this is so fucking hot. You're so fucking hot."

"Make me come, Chris," I challenge him.

"Oh, I want to," he says, and he moves inside me faster.

The pressure is perfect now, and I'm panting and fisting the sheets in my free hand. My body is building and reaching, and my inner walls are beginning to swell around his cock. I'm so close.

He's fucking me so hard and so fast, and his thumb is fucking my ass just as hard and fast. God, it feels so good, and I'm panting harder now.

I'm so ready to have my fluids dripping down my thighs, so I let go of the sheets and my clit and move my hands up to my breasts. I pull on my nipples hard, over and over. And that does it. I'm coming, releasing my fluids all over him and me.

And Chris follows right along with me, coming as I'm coming. He grunts and slams into me, and then stops all movements. He withdraws his thumb and his cock, and then he collapses on the bed, lying on his back.

I stand up. I'm ready to go. "Thanks for the orgasm, Chris."

"Anytime," he says. "And thank you," he adds.

I smile at him, and then I begin collecting my clothes. They're not soaking wet anymore, but they're not exactly dry either. They're damp, but I don't care. I just need to get home, because staying would imply that there's more between us than there really is. And I can't have that happen. So I clean myself up and get dressed.

I lightly brush my lips over Chris's, as he's right where I left him on his bed. His eyes are closed, and he's breathing even. I know he's probably not moving anytime soon. He's basically asleep already. So I give him a light and quick peck on his lips.

"See you around, Chris."

"Okay," he says sleepily, and then he begins snoring.

I let myself out, and I turn the lock on his doorknob right before I close the door. I don't know when he'll be up to lock the deadbolt, and I don't want to leave his door unlocked. So at least one of the locks is locked.

I exit his apartment building and step out into the rain. I shield myself with my umbrella and try to get home as fast as I can without falling down, and my mind is racing with thoughts the entire way. I need to end my friendship with Chris, but how?

One Night

Sometimes, I wish I felt more for Chris. He's a good man. He's kind, respectful, and handsome, but that swooning chemistry I long for just isn't there for me. And in truth, I don't think I've ever experienced potency like that before at all with any man.

Chris has been my fuck buddy for a while, but before him, I was single in every sense of the word for a year and a half, not dating anyone, not fucking anyone, not even talking to the opposite sex. And that's because my last boyfriend was a total asshole. And when I broke it off with him, I decided to stay away from men and just do me. So that's what I did, focusing on my writing, and time went by, and then I met Chris. And now this is where I'm at.

I guess the only thing I can do is just be honest. It shouldn't be too difficult. I mean, he already knows where I stand. I just hope he understands and doesn't hate me.

I sigh as I step into my apartment. I just need to relax and go to bed. I pour myself a glass of wine. Then I take it with me to the bathroom and run a bubble bath, and once the tub is ready, I strip my damp clothes off and sink into the bubbles. I sip on my wine, and I lay my head back and clear my mind of the impending predicament for the rest of the evening.

I had a great night, a spectacular night. And that's where my mind stays, on my professional accomplishments, and hoping it only gets better from here.

Chapter Three

It's been a few weeks since I ended my relationship with Chris. I met up with him at the park around Michigan Avenue and explained myself. He said he understood and acted like everything was fine, but he left in a hurry, and his eyes told a different story, melancholy registering in them, as well as loss and defeat. I felt bad. I didn't want to hurt him, but it had to be done.

I stayed in the park for a while that day and I wrote and wrote. It was a nice release of emotions for me, and I created a couple new short stories, and they're really good. Sometimes, writing is like therapy for me, a way to right my mind through my work. But now I'm back to being single in every sense of the word, which I'm basically used to, and I'm going to embrace it with a smile.

And today is going to be a fun day that's worth smiling about. I'm in Hawaii with my sister and my best friend, and my parents are here, too. Abby's mother is getting remarried this evening to a free-spirited hippie. He's great and just what her mother needs in her life. I'm happy for her.

I'm only in Hawaii for one day really. I go back home tomorrow afternoon, so I intend to have the best time while I'm here. I'm on a beautiful island, and I'm down for anything.

"This is the life," Lacy says as she sips on her frozen daiquiri, laid out next to Abby and I at the bow of the boat.

Abby's mother and her soon-to-be stepfather have taken us, plus my parents, on a big boat to have some fun before they get married, which is only a few hours until they say I do.

My mom and Abby's mother have been the best of friends for years and years. They met at a pottery class when Abby and I were about three years old. They bonded and hit it off instantly, and my mom was there every step of the way when Abby's mother and father got divorced. We've all become family and Abby's like a sister to me, to Lacy, too. It's really cool, and the three of us girls are tight as hell.

Abby's father is very much still a big part of her life and always will be. He's a good man and a good father, but things just didn't work out between her parents, although they ended on good terms. My dad still talks to Abby's father and hangs out with him on occasion, and my dad has also become friends with Abby's soon-to-be stepfather. And no one finds it weird at all and there's no jealousy. We're all just one big, happy family.

"Yeah, it is," I agree as I bask in the late afternoon sun.

The three of us are in our bikinis, drinking frozen strawberry daiquiris, and taking in the sun's rays as we lie in its warmth and float through the North Pacific Ocean. It's a beautiful day, and I'm enjoying myself entirely.

"So I noticed that Chris showed up at Intoxication last night," Abby says.

"He did?" Lacy says incredulously.

"Yeah," I respond. "He did."

Last night, Friday night, I gave the crowd more of my erotic poetry, just like I've been doing every Friday night for weeks now. It's been going great, really great. The crowd gets bigger every week, and I've gained a bigger following, too. But last night was the first time that Chris showed up since I ended things with him. He didn't approach me, but he watched me all night. It was unusual to say the least.

"What did he say to you?" Lacy asks me.

"He didn't say anything. He didn't try to get my attention at all. He just listened, watched, and drank."

"That's strange," Lacy says.

"Really strange," Abby agrees. "For him to be so into you, I'm surprised he didn't try to talk to you."

"Yeah, and especially after hearing your poems, I'm sure he was all types of horny and just itching to be close to you," Lacy says.

"Yeah, I don't know. It was weird."

Lacy and Abby nod their heads in agreement, and then they take a drink of their frozen, a little heavy on the alcohol, beverages.

"How are you and Steve?" I ask Abby, changing the subject, and then taking a drink of my strawberry, alcoholic refreshment. Abby and Steve have been dating since they met at the bar on my debut night.

"Ooh, yeah, give us all the details," Lacy says.

Lacy, Abby, and I live together in a spacious three bedroom apartment, but we're hardly there all three of us at the same time. Our careers keep us all very busy, and someone's usually going as someone is coming. So now is a great opportunity to catch up with each other.

"We're good," Abby says, and she automatically blushes.

"Have you two had sex yet?" Lacy asks her.

As far as I know, Abby and Steve have been taking things slow, a little too slow if you ask me, and ridiculously too slow if you ask Lacy, but Abby likes to take her time and really feel a man out before she jumps in his bed. But once she makes the decision to sleep with a man, she is quite the sex kitten herself.

"Yeah, Abby, spill it," I say.

"We have," she says, and her blush deepens, turning a little bit redder. "Several times," she adds.

"Now that's what I'm talking about," Lacy says, smiling. "Is he good in bed? How's the sex?" she asks, her eyes widening in curiosity.

"It's written all over her face," I answer my sister's question before Abby even opens her mouth. "I'm assuming the sex is wonderful." I smile at Abby.

"It's amazing." She beams. "He's hitting spots inside me that I didn't even know existed."

"You found a man that knows what he's doing," Lacy says. "That's insanely hot," she adds. "I just love a man that can fuck me properly without direction, but it's also kind of fun teaching less experienced men how to fuck just right."

"I don't know about that, Lacy. Chris was someone that I had to teach how to fuck me right, and even then, I still had to play with myself in order to get off."

"That's because you just weren't that into him," Abby says.

"Exactly," Lacy agrees.

"Well, I haven't been too into anyone yet, I always have to help my orgasms along."

"Just look at it like this, you have to fuck a lot of frogs before you find your prince charming," Lacy says, and she's completely serious. It's the motto she lives by.

"It is kiss a lot of frogs, Lacy," Abby corrects her.

"Same difference," she says, smirking at Abby. "Just tap into some promiscuity and have fun," she tells me. "Let your little vixen come out in more than just your words and stories."

"I'll see what I can do." I take a nice drink of my daiquiri.

"Do you want to go swimming?" Abby asks us. "All this sex talk is making my mind wander to Steve, and I'm getting a little hot and bothered just thinking about him."

"Thinking about him or his cock?" Lacy says, smirking again.

"His cock," I say, guessing by the lingering blush that's deepening again on Abby's cheeks.

"Yeah, I'm guilty," she admits.

"Why didn't you bring him here to Hawaii?" Lacy asks her.

"Because, even though he and his cock are amazing, I still want to take things slow," she says, and then she takes a drink of her daiquiri.

"You do you, Abby," I tell her, smiling.

"Yeah, and mix your sexy with a little sin," Lacy adds.

"That sounds more like you and Savannah's mixture," she says matter-of-factly.

"That's true," Lacy agrees. "But mine's mixed with a lot more sin than Savannah's."

And after that statement, we all laugh. It's funny, but it's so very true.

"I have an idea," I say, rising to my feet. "Let's throw the inner tubes in the water, and then try to jump right into the hole."

"Better than just swimming," Lacy says, and rises to her feet.

"We're going tubing shortly, girls," Abby's mother informs us, happily shouting from her position at the stern of the boat. We all give her thumbs up with a big smile.

"Let's play around before the real fun begins," Abby says, rising to her feet.

And we all romp around in the vast ocean waters.

The ocean water was refreshing and a ton of fun, plus tubing was a great thrill. Everyone enjoyed it.

And after that, we all went to our hotel rooms to get ready for the outside, tropical wedding, which was very personal and intimate, with only a few handfuls of guests in attendance. It was beautiful, romantic, and sweet, and now the party has begun.

The reception is taking place right outside of our resort, out in the open, fresh air, overlooking the ocean and its glorious surroundings. There's a dance floor, a live band, and plenty of good food all around, plus drinks flowing continuously.

I'm wearing an irregular lace halter, split beach dress. It's basically a long, wrap-around skirt and a crochet-like halter top that ties around my neck. The top is white with crocheted sunflowers all around the bottom of it, resting right above my belly button. The skirt is a very light greenish-grayish color, and it clings around my bottom half nicely. I have on a couple of white gold toe rings with my feet in open-toe strappy sandals. My hair is simple, hanging down my back in big curls, and my makeup is light.

The party is in full swing, but I'm just sitting at a table close to the bar, sipping on a Long Island Iced Tea and watching, as everyone is having fun. I'm having a good time, but all of this is reminding me of what I'm longing and missing in my life.

But I'm not sad, I'm hopeful, and I'll keep doing me and live vicariously through my characters.

"Now, why is a beautiful woman sitting here all alone?" a low, deep voice says, coming out of the mouth of a very good looking man, like take my breath away good looking, as he appears at my table.

Tall, fit, tone body, strong jaw line, eyes to get lost in, and a smile to render me speechless, which it has, but only for a few seconds. He's wearing khaki pants and a white button down shirt. He's holding a beer in his hand and gazing at me intently.

"Hi," I say, looking up into his eyes and smiling at him.

"Care if I join you?" he asks.

"Not at all," I reply.

He pulls out the chair next to me, turns it slightly sideways, and takes a seat, leaving only a few inches to separate us. His proximity is compelling, and my entire body becomes keenly aware.

"I'm Carter," he says, his eyes smiling at me now.

Damn, his eyes. They're bright fucking blue, like sapphires. Yep, I'm definitely getting lost in his eyes.

"Savannah," I murmur.

"That's a beautiful name for a beautiful woman."

Damn, his voice. There's so much manly bass in it. It's so sexy, making the hairs on the back of my neck stand up.

"Thank you."

"You still haven't answered my question."

"What? Why I'm alone?"

He nods and takes a drink of his Hawaiian beer.

I shrug. "Maybe I like being alone."

"I can understand that, and there's nothing wrong with that. I happen to be good at being alone."

"It's the best way to get to know one's self."

"I agree," he says. "And have you discovered who you are, Savannah?"

Ooh, just keep saying my name.

"Yes, I have," I reply. "And you?" I take a long sip of my strong, alcoholic concoction.

"I'd like to think so, although I'm still somewhat discovering things."

"Always a work in progress, forever evolving, embracing changes, and moving forward," I state.

"Exactly," he says, smiling. "You're very intuitive."

"Maybe, or maybe we just happen to be on the same page."

He stares into my eyes for a long minute, as if he's searching them, saying nothing, and then he takes a long drink of his beer. It's pretty intense for several, several seconds.

My heart rate quickens a little as I lose myself a little more in his eyes, and then he finally breaks the charged silence. "Because we both understand our need for independence and our need of solitude," he says.

"Yeah," I murmur. Damn, who is this man, and where did he come from? He's not getting personal with me, yet I feel like he already knows me.

"We have specific standards, and we set rules in place to achieve those standards," he says.

"Setting goals and striving to meet them," I add.

"Knowing that you are in charge of your happiness and what you want out of life," he says.

"Yeah," I murmur, enthralled by him.

"Never settling," he says.

"No, never," I agree.

"Dreaming of meaningful, powerful connections," he says.

"All the time," I admit.

"Because at the end of the day, that's all that really seems to matter," he says.

"Yeah," I murmur, and then I bite my bottom lip slightly. This man is reading my mind, somewhat tapping into my very essence.

His eyes drop to my mouth, and then quickly come back to my eyes. "But still welcoming the peace and silence and dwelling in the seclusion," he says. "Because that's who we are," he adds.

"You seem to be the intuitive one," I state.

"Maybe we both are." He smiles.

I smile back at him, and then I take a drink of my Long Island Iced Tea. He takes a drink of his beer, keeping his eyes on me.

"So tell me, Savannah, are you enjoying your time in Hawaii?"

Damn, his voice. He said my name again. I'd like him to moan my name. Shit, what am I thinking? I don't do one-night stands. But there are exceptions to every rule, right? Damn. No, I couldn't. I shake those thoughts out of my head and continue to stare into his eyes.

"I am. It's a beautiful island, but this wedding is kind of reminding me..." I pause, not really sure if I should say what's at the tip of my tongue.

"Of how solo you actually are," he finishes my sentence, and it is spot on.

I nod.

"Weddings have a way of doing that," he says, and then he sighs, and I'm pretty sure it's because we're still on the exact same page. He's not just reading my mind, he feels the same way. And then I notice a little sadness in his eyes, but he turns his head quickly toward the people on the dance floor. "But weddings also have a way of bringing out the love and affection between two people," he says. "For instance, look at that couple all over each other. They've probably been together for a couple decades, but they're still crazy about one another."

My eyes follow to the couple he's referring to, and I can't help it, I start laughing. "Those are my parents," I tell him. My parents are being very touchy-feely as they bump and grind on the dance floor.

"Really," he says, and turns his head back toward me, raising his eyebrows.

I nod and smile.

"Well, you have very cool parents," he says, smiling.

"Yeah, they are," I agree.

"So your family's here, you all must be very close to either the bride or the groom."

"Both actually," I offer. "How about you, are you a friend of the bride or the groom?"

"I'm not a guest," he states. "I'm just getting away."

"Cool." He's crashing the wedding. I like that. It's impulsive.

"So, how long are you here for, Savannah?"

Damn, that voice and my name together is a heady combination. Maybe I really should bend my rules just this once. Maybe...

"Just one day, I leave tomorrow."

"Same here," he says, and then he sighs again. Jesus, what is going on inside his head? But my question dissipates as he starts to speak. "I have to be honest with you," he begins, but pauses for a couple seconds and just stares at me, his eyes searching mine, but looking for what, I don't know. Then he begins again, "I'm fighting a strong urge to be with you all night."

Whoa. My inner vixen, who I usually only let out when I'm writing, speaking my poetry, or masturbating, stretches from her slumber and opens her eyes, fully ready to come out and do whatever this man has in mind.

Shit, I said I was down for anything on this island, so fuck it, my sexy could use some more sin mixed in with it. I can do one night. And with the way I'm responding to him inside and out, it promises to be a great night.

"Let's get out of here," I suggest.

"Really," he says, his eyes looking at me quizzically.

"Yeah, come on." I rise out of my chair, and then he does the same. "Are you down for some risqué fun?" I ask him.

"I'm definitely intrigued," he says, and he takes my hand.

And in that moment, my entire body is consumed by a spreading fire. And I'm fairly positive that it travels through us both as he threads his fingers through mine, because we both nearly gasp at the contact.

Whoa. My inner vixen is already stripping all of her clothes off and spreading her legs wide.

"What is that?" he says, confirming my thoughts.

"It's a preview of our night together. Come on."

We begin walking, and I take him to a secluded place on the beach that I noticed earlier today. There is a small cliff that we hop down, and that's the spot. There are big stones along the sand and absolutely no one around. It's just me, Carter, and the ocean.

I take my sandals off and start removing my clothing.

"What are you doing, Savannah?" he asks me, not taking his eyes off me at all. In fact, his eyes are roaming up and down my body and blazing with hot fire.

"Having fun," I say, and I remove my top. Now I'm standing before him in just my white, silk thong.

"Jesus, Savannah, you're gorgeous, so completely and utterly gorgeous."

"Thank you." I smile, and I start walking toward the water. I step into the waves and keep going. "Take your clothes off, Carter. Have some fun," I tell him, turning in the water to look at him. And to my pleasant surprise, he's already unbuttoning his shirt.

He takes his clothes off, watching me as I watch him, until he's standing in just his boxer briefs. And he is totally gorgeous as well, a finely sculpted and chiseled body with a tight ass six-pack to match. Damn, he is yummy. I bite my bottom lip as he walks my way.

He enters into the waves, and as he gets closer to me, I begin splashing him with water. He smiles at me and begins splashing me back. And we play around with each other, splashing and swimming. The water is warm, and the moon is glowing over the ocean, silhouetting our bodies against the waves as they crash into us. Skinny dipping is fun until our skin comes in contact again, and then the fire returns.

"Come back to my room with me," he murmurs close to my ear as he's behind me with his arms around my waist.

My entire body is lit up, and my inner vixen is panting.

"I don't really do one-night stands," I inform him.

"I don't either," he says.

I turn in his arms and look up into his eyes. "But there is no denying the attraction between us."

"I can't fight the urge any longer," he says. "There has been a force pulling me to you since the moment I set my eyes on you."

Whoa. This just got even more interesting.

And before I can form any words in response, he's lowering his lips to mine and crushing me against his body.

The air crackles with extreme sexual desire and swarms all around us, and I'm automatically assured that this is where I'm supposed to be.

His lips are soft and pressing against mine perfectly. I throw my hands into his caramel hair and slip my tongue into his mouth. He moans, and then I moan. And then our tongues start tasting each other.

We're both releasing potent pheromones. They're coursing through our bodies, spilling out of our pores, and mixing together in a way I've never experienced before. And he doesn't feel like a stranger at all. It feels right. He feels right.

Carter pulls his lips off mine, but I can tell he's reluctant, and so am I. We're both breathing hard, and then he presses his forehead against mine. "Will you spend the night with me?" he asks me.

"Yes," I whisper.

He kisses me and takes my hand in his, the fire being exchanged back and forth between us, and then we exit the ocean.

He places his shirt around me, and I put my arms through the sleeves, buttoning it up as he collects our shoes and clothing. Then he threads his fingers through mine again and leads me back to the resort, and very speedy, too.

And the air crackles the same hot passion and swarms all around us as we hurry to uncharted territories.

Chapter Four

Carter opens the door to his hotel room, and we enter. He sets down our clothing, walks to the patio, pulls open the curtains and blinds, and opens the sliding door, so that the warm night breeze blows through the screen. The moon shines into the room, lighting up the darkness in a romantic glow. And we can hear the sound of the waves crashing back and forth as the tide rises and falls with the ocean current. The mood is set, and he's looking at me expectedly.

There's an electric spark filling the room, and we aren't even touching. It's overwhelming me entirely, but my inner vixen is taking charge and already many steps ahead of me, deliciously fingering herself; which is adding to the heat between my thighs as it threatens to drip down my legs. So I unbutton his shirt and let it fall down my back, and then I remove my thong, stepping out of it with my eyes on his. He gasps, his eyes turn a darker shade of blue, and his cock stiffens in his boxers. And his reaction causes my arousal to begin dripping down my upper thighs. My body has never responded this way before. God, I'm ready to come all over this man.

"It's just one night," he says, sounding more like he's trying to convince himself.

"One hot night," I correct him.

"With no strings attached," he adds.

"None," I assure him. After tonight, we'll go our separate ways. So it's a good thing that I don't know any personal information about him, not even his last name. I don't want to know, because we'll never see each other again. It's just a hot encounter.

I take a few steps and close the distance between us. I look up into his eyes and stick my fingers into the seam of his boxer briefs, and then a blazing heat engulfs us, making me drip down my thighs some more, and causing his breath to catch in his throat. It's going to be a definite night to remember, but I'm not sure if that's good or bad.

He swallows hard. "It's been a while since I've been with a woman," he murmurs.

"I won't bite." I yank down his boxers, and his erection springs to life. His cock is long, thick, and already pulsating. I lightly move my hand up and down it, my breathing already a little uneven, and his breathing begins to get rough. "Unless you want me to," I add.

"Jesus, Savannah," he murmurs, and then he grabs my hips, and rather aggressively, pressing his fingers into my skin and making it sear. "I want you to," he tells me, and then his lips are on mine.

He kisses me with an urgent need, his lips strong on mine and filling my mouth with his tongue, allowing me to taste his desire as he urgently backs us into the bed, quickly lowering us onto it. He's between my legs with his cock rubbing against my sex. It feels so fucking good, and he's not even inside me yet.

He moves his hands to my face, holding my mouth to his and caressing my cheeks. Then he begins thrusting his hips into me, grinding against me, and his cock starts moving through my wetness, sliding between my folds and up to my clit. And I grind against him too as I grip the bedding in my hands.

Damn, this friction between our bodies is enough for me. It's so, so enough for me. I don't even need to touch my pussy or play with it at all. Carter is enough. But damn, Carter isn't mine. And fuck it, my body doesn't care. I begin moaning into his mouth and dripping so much more. Well, tonight he's mine. At least my pussy thinks so.

He pulls his lips off mine and stares into my eyes. "You're so wet," he says hoarsely.

"For you," I breathe, and I kiss him.

He groans on my lips and deepens our kiss once again, and then my body starts vibrating underneath him. This man is going to make me come, and nothing's happened yet.

I begin moaning nonstop into his mouth, and then he pulls back, saying nothing, breathing hard, and watching me come apart.

I cry out loudly and throw my head back, fisting the bedding now as my legs shake and my orgasm flows out of me.

"Oh fuck, you are so hot," he says. Then his body starts vibrating on top of mine. He moans fairly loudly, and then squirts his orgasm all on my sex and right above it.

My inner vixen sucks on her sticky, cream coated fingers, her legs still spread wide, completely ready for more.

"I can't believe you made me come like that," I say, my voice very breathy.

"Yeah, me either. I wasn't intending for you to come like that, or me, but it felt so good, and I just couldn't stop myself."

"I'm glad you didn't stop." I smile. He smiles, too.

He looks down at the mess he made on me, and then brings his eyes back to mine. "I'm sorry. I'll go get a towel," he says.

"No, I've got it." I take two of my fingers and wipe up his come with them. Then I stick my fingers in my mouth and suck them clean, and I stare into Carter's eyes as I do.

"Oh fuck, Savannah. You..... That..... God, you're so fucking hot."

"I want you to fuck me, Carter." His cock is still hard as he hovers over me, and I'm impressed. I've never been with a man that could stay rock hard after coming. Maybe it's from watching me taste his nut, or maybe it's just because of the intense attraction between us, but either way, it's fucking great.

"You're an amazing and wild woman," he says. "Skinny dipping, your mouth, and you seem to have a kinky way about you, don't ever change."

I bite my bottom lip as he pushes the head of his cock inside my soaking wet pussy. He gasps and stills, looking down into my eyes. He brushes his thumb over my bottom lip, and I release it, my bottom lip now very warm from his touch.

"You feel so good already," he says, his voice becoming hoarse again.

"Fill me with your big cock and make me come all over it." I wrap my body around his.

"Oh fuck," he calls out, and his whole body shivers as he pushes the rest of his cock inside me.

And my body becomes flushed all over as he fills me full.

The air sizzles all around the room and explodes into a raging inferno as our bodies connect on this intimate level. Damn, it's the exact type of shit I write about, and now I'm actually experiencing it on a very personal level of my own. I'm truly in ecstasy already.

Carter drops his lips to mine and begins pushing his cock in and out of me at an exquisitely nice pace, not fast, not slow, but just right. My pussy latches onto his cock as he slips his tongue into my mouth, and we both moan into the kiss. I move my hands into his hair and start meeting his every thrust, throwing my pussy back at him every time he pushes inside me and possesses me. And I never would've known that it's been a while since he's been with a woman, because he knows precisely how to fuck. God, it's like he jumped right out of one of my stories.

He pulls his lips off my mouth, leaving both of us gasping and panting, desperately needing air to our lungs. He stares into my eyes and doesn't blink. It's undeniably the most intimate and personal act between us up to this point. And it makes me wetter all around him.

"Savannah," he whispers, and I bite my bottom lip and squeeze him tighter, and then my inner walls begin pulsing around him, which makes him throb in my wet warmth.

God, hearing my name come out of his mouth as we're naked, eyes locked, and bodies glued together is going to send me completely over the edge. I am so close.

His mouth finds my breast, and his hand finds my ass. He devours my nipple and the surrounding area, and he digs his fingers into my backside, pulling on my ass cheek, causing his cock to fill me even more, which I didn't know was possible. Goddamn, his cock feels incredible, and he feels so strong and capable in my grip. I'm going to jump over the edge and right into total bliss.

"Oh... Carter..." I moan. And his whole body shivers.

He brings his eyes back to mine, and my insides latch around his cock even tighter. "Savannah," he whispers.

"Oh..." I moan. "I'm coming," I murmur, digging my fingers into his back, squeezing my thighs against him, and quivering in his arms.

My orgasm covers him in warm, thick cream, and he keeps pushing in and out of me, and he's grunting now with every thrust. And then I feel him throb really hard inside me, all the way inside me.

He growls his moans and empties his yummy cream deep inside me. "Savannah," he whispers very hoarsely. Then he collapses on me, but only for a minute, and then he's pulling out of me and rolling off of me.

The room is insanely hot, almost as if the heat was on and blowing through the vents. But it's just us. This heat has been following us around ever since he sat down at my table, and I like it. I like it a lot. So I let my eyes close and take the flames into my dreams with me.

*   *   *   *   *   *   *   *

I wake to the sun shining brightly and to the sound of the ocean waves crashing together. And there's a warm breeze touching my body, and I feel warm everywhere. But when I open my eyes, I discover that I'm alone in Carter's bed of his hotel room. I don't hear him in the room at all, but there's definite evidence of what transpired between us last night. Our creamy come is staining the bedding in a couple of areas, and recalling those memories brings a smile to my face.

"Carter," I call out, but there's no answer.

I sit up and stretch, and then I exit off the bed. I search the room for him, but he's gone, and there's no luggage anywhere.

I can't believe this. He ditched me.

He fucked me. He slept next to me. Then he ditched me, but probably not too long ago though. I can see his body's imprint on the bedding, the bedding that we fucked on top of and slept on top of. Damn, he put it on me like no other man ever has, which made me change my mind, and I was going to ask him his last name and get his number. Shit.

Well, this sucks, but I don't regret giving myself to him. It was beyond amazing, and I'll probably think about it every time I touch myself.

Just then, there's a knock on the door. I grab a robe, slip it on my naked body, and then answer the door.

"Good morning, Miss," a hotel staff member says. "I have breakfast for you, from the gentleman that stayed in this room." He pushes in a tray of food.

Okay, this is weird. "Thank you," I tell him. "How long ago did the gentleman leave?" I ask him before he exits the room.

"About thirty minutes ago, and he was in a hurry," the staff member says.

What the hell? He ditched me, but made sure breakfast was delivered. I'll have to ask Lacy how one-night stands are supposed to work, but I don't think it's like this.

"Okay, thanks."

"My pleasure, Miss, have safe travels," the staff member says, and then exits the room.

I look at the tray of food, and I see a small note with my name on it. I open it and it reads...

Savannah

Thank you for last night. It was amazing. You are amazing. But I had to leave. I'm sorry. I hope that you get home safely.

Damn. I have a lot of questions for Lacy.

Chapter Five

I sat in Carter's room for longer than I intended to, and I ate the breakfast of scrambled eggs, toast, and assorted fruit that he had sent to me. I just couldn't bring myself to leave. It was like something was trapping me in his room and begging me to stay for a while. So I did.

I could still smell him. I could still feel him. And everything we did and said to each other kept playing over and over in my head. It made my body heat all over again. And my inner vixen already had him on repeat in her domain and acted accordingly, touching herself and whispering for me to do the same. So I did.

I climbed back on the bed and lied in the spot he slept in, and his scent flooded my nostrils, and then I was engulfed in flames and already starting to drip. It felt like he was all over me, and I came so hard just from my fingers, my fingers teasing my sex and my nipples. And his name escaped my lips, causing my eyes to pop open in surprise. That's when reality truly set in, and I quickly gathered my clothes and ran out of his room, ignoring the intense pull that wanted me to stay.

I ran to my room so fast, and I immediately went to the bathroom and turned the shower on. The warm water and soap washed away all the evidence that I was with him, but my insides, especially my sex, are forever marked. My soul and my core both now feel alone, more alone than they ever did, and I don't know how to make it stop. But I'm not sure if I want it to stop, because like I said, I don't regret giving myself to him.

Still though, I'm so confused. I enjoyed myself immensely, and I would be with him again in heartbeat if he was here right now, but I wanted to rid my body of all traces of him, and I don't know why. This has never happened to me before.

I need Lacy.

Now clean and dressed, I go in search of my sister, and I find her and Abby sunbathing on the beach.

"There she is," Abby says, looking relieved. "Where have you been?" she asks me as I take a seat in a beach chair next to her and my sister.

"I told you I saw her take off with a really hot guy last night," Lacy says, answering Abby's question before I do. "Isn't that right, Little Vixen?" she says to me.

"It's true," I reply.

"And, did you mix some sin with your sexy?" Lacy asks me.

"I did."

"Savannah, you had a one-night stand?" Abby says, and a little too loudly. Luckily, there's not really anyone paying us any attention.

"Yes." And before I can say anything else about it, Lacy excitedly interrupts me.

"Details, I need lots of details," she says, smiling.

And before she bombards me with question after question, I start talking. "Okay, okay, let me first start off by saying that there was something potent and powerful in the air that surrounded us from the moment he sat down next to me, and it followed us and circled us all night."

I tell my sister and Abby everything from last night, starting with the conversation that Carter and I had, to the fun we had in the ocean, to the sexy and amazing time we had in his room. I give them all the details as they flood my mind. And as I talk about him and us, the images filling my mind with picture after picture, my insides begin to warm up yet again.

"It was amazing." I smile. "He made me come twice. He did. Him, just him, not me helping along and touching myself, nope, I was in complete ecstasy and gripping the bedding because of him, and him alone."

"Wow," Abby murmurs. "I can't believe you had sex with a stranger."

"I know. It's not my normal style, but I just couldn't resist him."

"Well damn, Little Vixen. Now I can call you that all the time, and not just because of your poetry and stories, but because you got sinfully sexy last night," Lacy says, and then she winks at me.

I smile at her.

"So you stayed the entire night with him. Did you have breakfast with him, too?" Abby asks me.

"Or did he have you for breakfast?" Lacy says, and she has a mischievous yet playful look in her eyes.

"Um, that is where the story gets weird," I say.

"What do you mean?" Abby inquires.

"Yeah, how does it go from deep conversation and strong attraction, to fun, to sinning all on his bed, to weird?" Lacy says.

"Well, maybe you can tell me, Lacy, because I'm not exactly sure what the protocol is for one-night stands."

"Alright, I'll do my best. What happened?"

"When I woke up this morning, he was gone, completely gone, luggage and all."

"Damn, that's messed up," Abby says, slightly shaking her head back and forth.

"He just took off while you were sleeping?" Lacy says, looking a little confused.

"Well, it was right before I woke up, like thirty to forty minutes or so before I woke up."

"And how do you know that?" she asks me, raising an eyebrow.

"Okay, this is where the story gets even weirder," I state. Abby and Lacy are both staring at me, and I continue. "A gentleman from the hotel staff came to the room with breakfast."

"What the hell?" Lacy voices a little loudly as she interrupts me.

"Shhh, Lacy, let her finish," Abby says.

"The staff member said that Carter ordered me breakfast, but then he left in a hurry."

"What?" Lacy exclaims.

I tell Lacy and Abby about the note that came with my breakfast, and then I tell them everything that happened after that. I don't get interrupted anymore, and I take them through my whole morning, recalling everything that led me up to this point, including everything I was feeling as well.

"I should've left his room after the hot sex. I don't even make it a point to stay the night with a fuck buddy, but I just felt so right being with Carter. It felt right. He felt right. And I felt like it was exactly where I needed to be."

"There's nothing wrong with staying the entire night with a one-night stand. Granted, I don't make it a habit to do that though. Too many emotions can be at risk. And one can get the wrong impression. But I did do it once," Lacy says.

"With Johnny," I state.

"Yeah," she replies. Johnny is her most recent ex-boyfriend. She met him while she was out having some fun, and she ended up going home with him. They were basically together every day after their first night, but then he cheated on her, so now she's single.

"I guess it is good you didn't get too personal with him," Abby says, and she takes a drink out of her water bottle that's next to her.

"Maybe so, Abby, but if she would've gotten his last name and where he's from, then she could hunt him down and bitch him out for taking off," Lacy says.

"Well, that's true," Abby agrees. "But maybe he has a good excuse. He did leave her a note and apologize."

"Yeah, but I'm never going to see him again," I say, feeling a little empty inside.

"I'm sorry, Savannah," Abby says, her eyes full of sympathy.

"The one time I actually find a man that's spontaneous and we have explosive fireworks and untamed passion between us and it ends up being too good to be true," I say, shaking my head.

"Yeah, I'm sorry, Savannah," Lacy says, her eyes full of sympathy, too.

"Plus, he's left his mark on me," I state. "I can still hear his voice, feel his touch, and smell his scent, especially when I talk about him or think about him, and it's even more evident every time I close my eyes."

"I know you probably don't want to hear this, but the best way to get over someone is to get with someone else," Lacy tells me.

She's right. That's not what I want to hear.

"Yeah well, I'm not having anymore one-night stands or anymore fuck friends for that matter. I'm just going to channel all of my emotions and feelings into my work."

"I get it," Lacy says. "But don't let what happened prevent you from having fun, especially some sexy fun."

"I'll try." I give them both a small smile.

"Well, I'm excited to read whatever story you come up with after this. I know it will be great," Abby says, smiling.

"That's true," Lacy says. "You could end up with a best seller from this situation."

"That would be cool." My smile gets a little bigger and brighter.

"Let's go for one last swim before we leave this island," Abby suggests.

"Sounds good," Lacy agrees.

"Okay," I agree, too.

I pull my sundress over my head, as my bikini is already on me, and I follow my sister and best friend into the ocean. And we enjoy the water until it's time to go to the airport.

*   *   *   *   *   *   *   *

I get comfortable in my window seat, resting my head back with my headphones on and listening to a collection of Tori Kelly songs. But as the plane ascends, flying higher and higher, my feelings of loneliness begin to overwhelm me, making me feel more alone than I ever have in all my life. And I feel like a big piece of me has been left in Hawaii, never to be found again.

Chapter Six

"Oh, Carter, again," I beg in-between my heavy panting.

I'm on all fours, and he slams into me again, smacking my backside repeatedly while his other hand grips at my backside roughly. He's fucking me like he owns me, and we're both watching it all unfold, as we're on my bed positioned directly in front of my mirror. God, it's so hot, and it feels great.

Our eyes are locked on each other's in our reflection, which makes me so much wetter. My juices are actually dripping out of me every time he withdraws his cock, even when he pulls back just a little. Then when he thrusts back into me, his balls smack against my sex, slightly hitting my clit, and his balls are wet, very wet with my juices. And that is so hot, too, along with feeling so good.

Carter moves his hands up to my breasts and squeezes them over and over. Then he bends over my back, so that his mouth is close to my ear, and his quiet moans fill my eardrum. He holds my gaze in the mirror, tugs on my nipples, and continues to thrust into my sex. His actions and his movements are so precise, asserting me to him. And his hushed vocals are like music notes in my ear, sending waves of pleasure to my sex. But those eyes, his bright blue gems are taking me back to the North Pacific Ocean, and I no longer feel alone.

"You are mine, Savannah," he declares at my ear, his eyes still locked on mine. He tugs my nipples harder. "Mine," he growls, then bites my earlobe.

"Oh yes, yours Carter, yours," I reply, my words pronounced through a series of husky breaths.

He bites my earlobe again, and then whispers, "Mine," directly in my ear.

"Yes!" I exclaim, and I come hard, so very hard, dripping all over Carter's cock and down my thighs to the sheets below us.

"Oh, Savannah," he loudly moans, and my eyes pop open.

I'm wide awake, taking deep breaths, and lying in the aftereffects of my wet dream.

Jesus, every night my dreams get more vivid, more real, and more intense, I think to myself.

It's been two months since my hot encounter in Hawaii, and I've been dreaming of Carter every single night. Every dream is different, every scenario is different, but the actions and outcomes are always the same, Carter fucking me so properly, and me always coming right before my eyes open. I wake up every morning soaking wet, breathless, and alone.

And since my nights are dominated by desire, I've been using that as fuel to push forward each day. I've been spending all of my time writing nonstop. The only time I really leave my apartment is to go to Intoxication every Friday night and recite my poetry.

I've written more poetry, too, plus two more short stories, and I've been working on my novel. The two short stories I wrote are a direct result of my one-night stand. They're really good, and Lacy and Abby both agree.

I've also taken the time to finally publish all my short stories. I have a total of ten of them, and they all contain three parts to the story and are about seventy five pages each, so they are classified as novellas. They've only been published for two weeks, and they're already selling really well. It's exciting.

It's Friday, and I will be reciting two more erotic poems this evening. But first, I need to get through the day, starting with breakfast, right after I change my panties. I should probably change my sheets, too, but maybe I'll soak them a little more after I write.

I slip on a clean thong and head to the kitchen.

"Hey, you're up early," I say to Lacy. She's usually a late sleeper since my parents' store doesn't open until eleven.

"Yeah, I'm having breakfast with Brian," she says, smiling.

"Who's Brian?" Sometimes, it's hard to keep track of Lacy's love life.

"I met him yesterday when I went and grabbed some brunch before opening the store. He was entering the restaurant at the same time as me and picking up a carryout bag as well. We started talking as we were waiting for our food, and he paid for my meal. Then he asked if I would join him in the park to eat with him. I agreed. Savannah, he's hot as hell."

"So, did you have sex yet?" I don't know who she was with, but she went out last night, and I wouldn't be surprised if it was with him and they had sex. Sex is usually the first thing that Lacy gets out of the way. She likes to know what a guys packing before she gets too involved.

"Well actually, we kind of did," she says, still smiling.

"What does that mean?" I begin gathering the items out of the fridge to make an egg sandwich, and I start cooking my breakfast.

"The conversation between us was effortless. It just flowed and flowed. Then he kissed me, and I felt him everywhere. And when he released my lips, he asked if he could taste me."

"Damn, that's audacious, but I understand the feeling of feeling a man light you up all over. So, he gave you oral right in the park?" Now that shocks me.

"Yes, but there was no one around, and we were in a somewhat secluded area that had lots of trees everywhere."

"Wow," I state. "Well, it must have been good. You're actually waking up early for a man. That's not like you."

"It was more than good. He made my whole body quiver." She grabs her keys.

"Damn, that's really hot."

"It was so hot, and because of that, I was a little late opening the store," she confesses.

"How late," I inquire.

"Just twenty minutes," she says.

"Well, your secret is safe with me."

"Thanks." She starts walking to the door. "I'll see you later tonight," she says, and opens the door.

"Bye. Have fun," I say, and giggle under my breath.

"I will," she happily replies, then leaves out the door and closes it behind her.

I take a seat in front of my laptop, turn it on, and begin eating.

But the last sex scene that I wrote is staring me in the face, as steamy words are all over the screen, and as if they were in all caps and bold fonts. And dammit, it's causing my brain to send flashes of my dreams of Carter through my mind. Damn.

My pussy is tingling, and my inner vixen is already on top of her red, silk sheets with her legs spread wide, and she's begging me to do the same.

"No," I murmur, and squeeze my thighs together.

Fuck, I go through this every morning, fighting the urge to let my mind and body have its way. I fight the dreams of Carter, the memories of him, and the thoughts of him, just fighting the urge to let him consume me and masturbate.

Like I said, I use all of those desires to fuel my writing. But I do give in occasionally and masturbate to my memories of Carter from our one night. How can I not?

But it's not how I thought it would be.

I knew I would think about him every time I touched myself, but it's been affecting me way more than I ever imagined it could or would. It makes me want him more and more.

So every day I fight the battle within me and just write. And I hope that with time that my night in Hawaii will just be a distant memory that lies dormant in my mind. I really hope so, because I don't know how many more days I can continue like this.

I even spent a few hours one day thinking of how to go about getting his last name and where he's from. I contemplated hiring a private investigator to find him, but I quickly talked myself out of that. Because, who knows who he really is, or what I would actually discover if I found him. But part of me still wants to look into it.

I thought I could handle a one-night stand with him, but I was so wrong.

I push my empty plate aside and let my fingers hover over the keyboard, ready to stroke the keys and form some more sexy pages in this book.

*   *   *   *   *   *   *   *

"I never thought our relationship would enter into lust. I'm going to have to tell him the truth soon. I just hope he doesn't hate me." There, that chapter is done, I say to myself, and stretch out in my chair.

I've been writing for the past eight hours nonstop. Well, I stopped for a few minutes to put together a salad for myself, but I ate it as I wrote. I didn't want to completely stop writing just to eat, because the words have been flowing out of me since I made the first keystroke.

But now my eyes are starting to bug me from staring at the computer screen for so long, so I guess that's my cue to give my writing a rest for the day. I save my book and shut down my laptop. Then I stretch some more and let my eyes close.

Images of Carter on top of me and deep inside me fill my mind. "Shit," I breathe, and I open my eyes. I've had some majorly intense dreams and visions of Carter today. What is the universe trying to tell me?

My pussy is tingling more extreme now, and my inner vixen is already pushing a few fingers into her sex.

"Fuck it," I murmur. I'll let my mind and body have what they so desire.

I rise from the chair and go to my bedroom. Then I strip all my clothes off and climb onto my bed. I stare at my reflection in my mirror for a couple seconds, but quickly close my eyes instead. And the flashbacks begin.

I lie back on my pillows and let the cravings consume me. After all, it is what my mind and body both want. So I open my legs and place my hands on my breasts. I'm not using any toys this time around, just my hands and my fingers to touch myself.

My mind is showing me image after image of Carter and me and Carter and me. It's making me wet already.

I squeeze my breasts in my hands and moan as my mind shows me Carter sucking on my nipples, and he sucks them hard, going back and forth between each one, and looking into my eyes right before he envelops his mouth around my nipple each time. I can almost feel him doing it, too. The images are so clear and accurate, showing me every single detail that defines him.

I moan a little more consecutively, and I start tugging on my nipples. Then I start dripping onto the sheets. It's a good thing I didn't change them yet, because I know I'm going to leave another big wet spot. In fact, my entire sex is throbbing, and that makes me tug my nipples harder.

"Oh damn," I murmur. My mind is showing me Carter taking my nipple between his teeth and tweaking and pulling on it, one, and then the other.

"Oh shit, I going to come." I begin to absentmindedly grind into the mattress.

I squeeze my breasts and pull my nipples, and my orgasm pours out of me and onto the sheets. And I moan very loudly as powerful waves of pleasure take over.

Goddamn, a man that can make me come just from sucking and tugging on my nipples, it's what I long for, to come just from a man's steamy touch, the touch of his fingers or mouth or tongue, however he chooses to touch me, but just from his touch alone. But of course, it's too good to be true. I take a deep breath and blow it out.

And I'm about to open my eyes, but my mind presents me with another image of Carter. His finely sculpted body is on top of mine. He's staring down into my eyes as he moves his big, hard cock through my glistening pussy lips. It's just like our night in Hawaii, and I can almost feel his cock.

I move my hands down to my wet warmth and take two fingers from one hand and two fingers from my other hand and push them inside my pussy. I push them in deep and moan as I adjust to the feeling. God, it feels good.

And as I moan again, right as I begin pulling my fingers halfway out and pushing them back in, my mind delivers the image of Carter filling me deeply with his cock, just like our night in Hawaii. It's going to make me come again.

I don't know what my mind is trying to do to me, but I'm beyond the point of caring. I'm completely consumed, and I stuff my pussy with my fingers over and over.

I begin to absentmindedly grind into the mattress again, and I begin moaning nonstop.

My mind shows me his cock going in and out of me, like I'm watching a porno, but starring me and the man of mystery. And my fingers move inside me at the same rate and pace that his cock does in the image in my mind. It's making me soaking wet.

I can feel my orgasm at the tip of my fingers. I'm so, so close.

I push my fingers in and pull them halfway out. Then I push them inside me again, but hard and fast. Then I do it again, crying out loudly the second time, and I come. I come hard all over my fingers and the sheets.

"Oh shit," I breathe as my sex is still coming. This masturbation session has been so powerful, all of it, the images, the feelings, and both of my orgasms. "Shit," I breathe again. I'm still coming, wetting the sheets a lot, and still lost in my own mind.

But I need to relax, so I slowly withdraw my fingers and take a few cleansing breaths in order to try and calm my body down. And as soon as I open my eyes, the images disappear, and my orgasm comes to a halt. "Damn," I breathe.

My body is coming down from its high finally, and I sink into the mattress. My eyes are coming down, too, starting to droop. I keep blinking them open, and every time they briefly shut, I get an image of Carter and I lying in bed with me held tight in his arms. It's nice, and I let my eyes stay closed with that image frozen in my mind, not changing and not disappearing.

Chapter Seven

I tip my head back, bring the shot of whiskey to my lips, and then let the liquid run down my throat. I'm sitting at the bar at Intoxication, and I'll be reciting my first of two poems tonight in just a little bit.

I haven't really been able to shake the masturbation session from earlier today out of my mind, and it's not really helping that I fell asleep for a little while after that either. I had more dreams of Carter, but I didn't have time to masturbate again. So I'm hot and bothered and feeling really horny. My performances tonight should be extra sexy because of it.

"Are you alright?" Abby asks me. She's sitting next to me and watching Steve pour drinks for the many, many customers that continue to enter the bar.

"Yeah," I reply. "Is it hot in here to you?" I pick up a small napkin and begin waving it back and forth in front of my face.

"Well, I might not be the right person to ask, because I am a little hot from watching my man." She turns her head back to her favorite bartender, and their eyes connect, and they both smile at each other.

"Right," I giggle, and then I fan her with my napkin. She starts giggling, too.

"It's still the aftereffects of Carter, isn't it?" she inquires after a few seconds, not giggling anymore and turning her head back to me. My giggles have stopped, too. And the heat dwelling inside me scorches a little more at the mention of his name.

"Yes," I murmur. I take a deep breath and blow it out, and then I begin fanning myself once again. "But today has been a lot more intense than the intensity that I am faced with every day."

"Damn," she says.

"Yeah," I agree. "I don't know why today is so extra, but I can feel him everywhere right now."

"Maybe Lacy is right. Maybe you should get with someone else and rid your mind of him once and for all."

"I can't believe you agree with her."

"I know," she says. "But it's been two months, Savannah. You've got to get past this, past him, and forget about him."

"Yeah, I know. I want all of the dreams, all of the flashbacks, and all of the memories to stop, but I can't bring myself to have another one-night stand."

"I can't believe I'm asking you this, but why?"

"Who are you, and where's my best friend?" I stare at her in disbelief. Abby would never have a one-night stand, so I'm a little shocked that she agrees with my sister.

"I wouldn't normally encourage you to have a one-night stand, but this is starting to get out of control, and I'm worried about you. So just humor, please."

"Okay. I'm worried that if I do it again that the same thing will happen, and then I'll be stuck with a mind that won't let me forget about two men."

"Oh," she murmurs. "That's not worth the risk then."

"Exactly," I agree.

"What about a double date with me and Steve? He has a few single, hot friends that I could hook you up with."

"Sure, it's worth a try."

And speaking of Steve... "Here you go, Savannah," Steve says as he approaches us, placing another shot of whiskey in front of me.

"Thanks," I tell him, putting a smile on my face.

"You're welcome. Good luck tonight," he tells me, returning a smile, but his is brighter than mine, showing his teeth.

"And for you, Baby," he says, placing a beer in front of Abby. He kisses her on the lips and lingers there for a minute. And she's blushing as he goes back to fulfilling drink orders.

I tip my head back and down my shot.

The MC takes the stage and grabs the Mic.

"Savannah, I know you already know this, but you look so freaking sexy. You'll probably end up with a few offers for possible dates before the night is over," Abby says.

I rise out of my seat. "Well, if they're hot prospects, then I'm open to that." I smile at her, and she smiles back.

Besides being extremely hot and bothered, I really feel incredibly sexy. I'm wearing a red pencil skirt that is a bandage mini skirt with a sexy high waist. My top is a matching red belly shirt with short sleeves, no v-neck, just a regular collar, like a t-shirt. I have on white open-toe heels. My hair is pulled up into a neat ponytail, the tail in one big, spiral curl, and my makeup is light tonight, just mascara and red lipstick. Red happens to be my favorite color, so yeah I'm definitely feeling very sexy.

"Ladies and gentlemen," the MC begins, "it's that time again. The sexy poetess is ready to seduce you with her words. But are you ready for her?"

The crowd, which is the biggest that it's ever been since I've been performing here, erupts into very loud cheering and clapping with a few whistles in the mix as well. It's great, and it gives me a little adrenaline boost, which smothers a little bit of the flames that are residing inside me.

"Here she is," the MC announces, "the beautiful, the sexy, the ever so talented, Savannah Lewis."

"Put them on the edge of their seats, Savannah," Abby whispers from behind me. I look over my shoulder and smile at her and wink.

The crowd continues with their boisterous welcoming, and I make my sexy walk slowly onto the stage. My walk is what starts my performance, so it has to be sexy and slow for the right affect. I take the Mic and wait for the crowd to quiet down.

"I love you, Savannah!" a guy in the audience shouts, and I spot him right away, close to the stage. He's in here every Friday night with his wife. He's a nice guy, and his wife is equally as nice, and she doesn't seem to mind his outburst. So I smile at the gentleman and wink.

The crowd begins to calm down. "Thank you," I speak into the Mic.

"I love you, too, Savannah!" a female shouts from the crowd.

"Well, thank you," I say into the Mic. "You all have made this my home on Friday nights. You are all amazing!"

"Savannah, Savannah, Savannah, Savannah," the entire audience chants my name, and it fills me with more adrenaline, further smothering some of the flames inside me. And after about a minute, everyone starts to quiet down.

And that cues the band behind me to start playing. They play a slow, instrumental piece of jazz music, which will continue as I speak my erotic words. It's perfect, setting the tone for my poetry. It's new to my performance, just implemented last week. It was my idea, and the audience loves it. I do, too.

"This poem is called, Gazing at Me. Are you ready for it?"

The crowd replies with hoots, hollers, and whistles, and I get right to it, staring at the mass of people and speaking slowly and seductively.

"Gazing at me
His eyes are burning flames
Gazing at me
With a want, with a longing, with a need
Gazing at me
I'm frozen where I stand
And I can't look away
Because I'm bewitched
I'm hexed by the potency of him
Gazing at me
And I'm dripping wet
Gazing at me
I'm waiting and ready
Gazing at me
And then he hurries toward me
Gazing at me
Like a predator, so hungry and so savage
Gazing at me
He crushes my body against his
Kissing me with luscious lips
Completely suffocating my kiss

As his adept fingers stroke my wet folds
And transports me to heavenly bliss
All from gazing at me"

The crowd explodes with praise, clapping, cheering, whistling, and most have jumped up from their seats. It's a wonderful feeling, bringing me glee and causing my lips to curl up in a big and bright smile.

"Thank you," I speak into the Mic, and everyone gradually begins to quiet down. "Most of you know the drill, and for those of you that don't, there's more, so stick around. I'll be reciting some more steamy poetry a little later this evening." The crowd cheers and whistles, and I wink at them and blow a kiss, and then exit the stage.

I sit down next to Abby at the bar. "You killed it once again." She smiles. Then she leans into my side and whispers at my ear, "Steve was behind me the whole time during your performance, and he was kissing on my neck, and also whispering in my ear how hot he was getting from your words. He wants your book of poetry, and so do I." She straightens back up in her seat.

"I haven't published my poetry," I say, just slightly puzzled, because she should know that.

"I know, but you really need to. I'm sure me and Steve are not the only ones that would like it in our possession."

"Yeah, you're probably right."

"You know I am," she says. "You pack this bar every Friday night, bringing more and more people in every week. They come to hear you speak, and they hang on every word."

"They do, don't they." I smile.

"Yep, you're the hottest thing in Chicago," she says, and she's serious.

"I wouldn't go that far."

"Oh, come on, Savannah. You and your words are so hot that your parents are even getting a ton more business, not that they needed the help."

"Well, you have a point," I agree. My parents' business does really, really well. It always has, but they are getting an abundance of new customers a lot more lately. "I guess I have another book to publish then." I smile.

"Yes, you do." She smiles.

Just then, I see, from the corner of my eye, Lacy approaching us, and she's holding a man's hand, and he's very hot. This must be Brian, unless my sister has another hottie she's playing with, which is totally possible.

"Hey, Lacy," I say, and smile.

"Hey, Little Vixen, hey, Abby," she says, smiling broadly.

"Hey, Lacy," Abby says, smiling.

"This is Brian," Lacy introduces us.

"Hello, ladies," he greets us, grinning. He lets go of Lacy's hand and extends his hand to me and Abby, and we each, in turn, shake his hand. He has a nice, firm grip. Then he takes Lacy's hand in his again. "It's Savannah, right?" he says to me.

"Yes," I reply.

"Lacy's told me a lot about you," he says.

She has? That's quite shocking. She just met this guy and is already opening up to him. Damn. He must be something special. Lacy doesn't let just any guy into her mind, maybe her bedroom on occasion, but not her mind.

"She's told me of your writing, your books, your poetry, and the nickname she calls you," Brian tells me. "And she's right. You're really good," he adds.

"Thank you," I say, smiling.

He turns his focus on Abby. "She's told me some about you as well, Abby."

"Really," Abby says, looking shocked.

"Yeah, you're her sister, too, the hot teacher."

"Lacy!" Abby blurts out, and she's blushing, and I'm giggling next to her.

Lacy smiles and shrugs her shoulders. "Well, it's true," she says.

"It is true," Brian agrees. "Don't be shy, Abby," he adds. "All three of you are hot, very beautiful."

"Oh, I like you, Brian. You better stick around," I tell him, then I wink at Lacy, and she smiles back.

"I plan on it," he says, grinning.

The band is playing a lot of upbeat music, music to drink to, music to dance to, basically music to party to. It's lively for sure.

"How about I spin you around on the dance floor, Sexy," he says to Lacy.

"I'd love to," she replies, smiling at him. Then he pulls her into the crowd.

"Wow!" Abby exclaims.

"Yeah," I agree. "He's hot, and he seems to have quite the affect on our promiscuous man-eater."

"A big affect," she says. And I get thrown off my square as a thought or maybe a realization comes to mind. "What is it?" Abby says, noticing my change in facial expressions I'm sure.

"I think the universe is fucking with me."

"What are you talking about?" she says.

"I'm in Lacy's shoes, and she's in mine."

"Oh!" she voices, and her eyes get big with the understanding.

"Yeah, I had the one-night stand, which is supposed to be her thing. And she has what seems to be an awesome guy, which is supposed to be my thing."

"The tables have definitely turned," she says.

"That double date with you and Steve is sounding really good right now."

"Great. I know just the..." She stops and stares over my shoulder, and she almost looks frozen.

"What?" I inquire.

And before she can open her mouth to speak, someone is tapping me on the shoulder, and he smells very familiar. "Savannah," he says, and I turn on my barstool. "Hi," he says, and flashes a quick grin at me.

"Chris, hi," I murmur, and whatever flames that were still blazing inside me are completely smothered now. Then a cold shiver runs down my back. Damn. My body has never reacted this way in his presence, but that just assures me that I did the right thing by leaving him alone.

But this is interesting. Since I ended my relations with Chris, he's still been coming to this bar, not every Friday night, but he still shows up every once in a while. And this is the first time that he's sought me out and spoken to me. It's definitely unexpected, but I'm a little curious as to what he's going to say to me.

"You're really moving up. It's great. I'm happy for you. Congratulations," he says, grinning.

"Thank you." I smile sweetly.

"And congrats on publishing your stories, I hear they're doing really well."

"Yeah, they are. Thank you."

Chris starts to open his mouth to say something, but he's cut off by a group of young women shouting my name and coming toward me. And it looks like they all have a book in their hands, some with more than one book. I wonder if they're mine. I would think that they most likely are. I mean, why else would these women bring books into the coolest bar in Chicago?

"Will you sign our books and take a picture with us?" one of the ladies asks me.

"Sure," I reply, smiling. "I'd love to."

"Well, I'll let you do your thing, Savannah. I just wanted to say hi and give you my kudos," Chris says. "I'll see yah around."

"Thanks, Chris. See yah." And he walks back into the crowd.

I give all my attention to the ladies holding my newly published novellas. "Are you enjoying yourselves this evening?" I ask them.

"Yes!" they all exclaim.

"We're big fans of yours," one of the ladies says, smiling very brightly.

"I have all your books," another of the ladies says, smiling just as brightly.

"I do, too," yet another one of the ladies says, wearing the same bright smile. "I love them!" And all the women nod their heads in agreement.

"Thank you." I smile at them. "So, what are your names?" I ask, and I grab a pen that's nearby off of the bar.

One by one, each lady tells me their name, and I sign their books, plus I leave a positive message. I write, "You make your life what you want it to be. Listen to your heart and always follow your dreams." It's the same inscription I write on the inside of anyone's book that they ask me to sign. Then I take a picture with each young lady individually, and then a group picture with them all. And after that, they excitedly merge back into the crowd.

Then some more people approach me, a few men and women. They ask me to sign their books and take pictures as well, and some are just interested in conversation. So I do my thing and interact with my fans. And that is the norm for the rest of the evening until it's time for me to get on stage again.

Even if the universe is set to fuck with me, this is still turning out to be a wonderful night. I feel accomplished and happy, and I'm ready to give these people what they came for, but I could use another shot first. So I grab the whiskey glass in front of me and tip my head back, swallowing the brown liquid in one gulp.

The MC takes the stage. "Ladies and gentlemen," he speaks loudly into the Mic. The crowd goes wild, knowing what time it is. "I like your enthusiasm," the MC says. "So without further ado, here she is, my favorite poetess and yours, Savannah Lewis." The crowd continues with their wild acclamation as I rise from my seat.

I walk my sexy strut onto the stage and grab the Mic, smiling out to the audience, and the band behind me begins to play a slow and sexy jazz instrumental. "Sex," I speak clearly, loudly, and sensually suggestively. A hush falls on the crowd. "Sex is natural. Sex is beautiful. Sex is so utterly hot." The crowd hoots, hollers, and whistles. "This is called, More."

> "More
> He kisses all my pink parts
> Further igniting the flame in my core
> Leaving me gasping
> And wanting more
> More
> He rips my panties
> He shreds them
> Watching the lace fall to the floor
> More
> He drops to his knees
> Tasting me
> Licking me
> Making me beg for more
> More
> Leaving me weak in the knees

I can hardly speak
His tongue
His fingers
Making me leak
More"

The crowd jumps from their seats, going wild with their applause and many cheers. "Thank you," I say into the Mic, and smiling into the crowd.

All of a sudden, I see an extremely hot and sexy man with caramel hair and sapphire eyes step out of the crowd and into my view. Our eyes lock, and the flames return with a red-hot fire that fills my insides everywhere.

Holy shit!

Carter?

Chapter Eight

Am I dreaming? This can't be real. I pinch myself and blink a few times. The minor sting travels to my brain, and my skin is left a little pink. Yep, I'm awake. This is definitely real.

I return the Mic to its holder, the crowd still giving me their praise, and I reluctantly pull my eyes off of the mystery man. I blow the audience a kiss and give them a wave, and then I exit off the stage, feeling those blue eyes on me the whole time.

He's here. He's really here. Has this been what the universe has been trying to tell me all day?

I walk back to the bar being followed by the heat and no doubt Carter as well. So I turn and face him, and the heat instantly swirls all around us. God, he looks mouth-watering good and smells just as delicious, and I'm beyond hot and bothered now.

"Carter," I breathe, staring into his eyes. "Hi," I murmur, getting lost in his eyes. I grab the edge of the bar.

"Hello, Savannah," he says, and grins at me. His voice is deep and sexy and giving me goose bumps. "You're brilliant, absolutely amazing." His smile widens.

"Thank you." And before I can say anything else, as I'm ready to interrogate this man, I notice a nice size group of people, mostly ladies, heading my way. They all look very animated, and they all have a book in their hands.

"Savannah!" they begin calling my name very loudly.

"You're very popular," Carter says.

"It seems that way," I observe.

"I would like to talk to you, Savannah, that's if you're willing and available to."

"I'd like to talk to you, too, Carter, as soon as I'm finished here, if that works."

"It does," he says. "I'll wait for you." He walks to the other end of the bar and takes a seat.

Hmm, if he really does wait, that's a good thing. I'm not sure how long I'll be, but I hope he does wait. There are so many unanswered questions, and there's unfinished business between us if you ask me, and if my body could talk, it would agree.

"Savannah, I love your poetry and your short stories," a college-age girl says to me, and she's smiling from ear to ear.

"Thank you." I smile at her.

"Me, too, and I can't wait for your novel," another college-age girl says to me.

"Well, that goes for you and me both," I tell her. Then I look at the entire group that's in front of me. "How are you all doing tonight? Are you having a good time?"

"We're having a great time!" one of the young ladies exclaims.

"Hell yeah," several of them agree.

"I'm not going to lie. My girlfriend had to drag me here tonight, and I'm glad she did. This bar is the place to be, and you are the one to see," a college-age man says to me.

"Well, I applaud your girlfriend. She's right. This is the bar to be at." And the girl next to the young man giggles a little bit. She must be his girlfriend.

"And you're the one to see," one of the young ladies says.

"Definitely," another girl says. "We all came here to hear you speak, and to try to get a chance to talk to you."

"Thank you." I smile. "You guys, my fans, are the reason why I keep writing." Then I lean in a little closer to them. "Plus, I love it, too," I add, and wink at them.

"It definitely shows," one of the girls says. "I can feel your passion every time I open up my Kindle to your stories."

"Yeah, same here," one girl says, and the rest of the group all nod their heads in agreement.

I smile warmly at them, just a bit speechless.

"Will you sign our books?" one of the girls asks.

"Of course," I reply.

"And take a picture with us?" another girls asks.

"You bet." I grab a pen off the bar and begin signing the inside cover of everyone's books.

I spend the next thirty to forty five minutes or so signing the novellas that I wrote, plus I take pictures with each and every person in this group, individually and group photos, too. The conversation we all shared was really nice and very rewarding, and I get a few hugs before they merge back into the crowd.

"Savannah," Abby begins as she appears by my side, "that guy at the other end of the bar seems to be watching you, and he's seriously hot."

"He is hot, isn't he," I reply, and then I look toward the other end of the bar and lock eyes with the seriously hot guy.

"Are you going to talk to him, or are you going to wait and see if he approaches you first?"

"Oh, I already know him," I tell her, and bring my eyes and attention back to her.

"Really," she says, looking at me quizzically.

"Well, I know his first name and how big his cock is," I say, correcting myself. "That's Carter."

"What!" she exclaims. "You're kidding, right?"

"No joke." I shake my head.

"Oh my god, what is he doing here? Does he live here?"

"I don't know anything yet, but I'm about to find out."

"Well, I can't wait to hear this," she says. "Be careful."

"I will."

"I'm staying at Steve's tonight. I'll see you tomorrow, and I'll be expecting details."

"Okay." I smile, and then I give her a hug.

"He's so hot, Savannah," she murmurs as I let her go.

"Yeah," I agree, and then I take a deep breath and blow it out, hopefully bracing myself for all the sexy sins of lust that I know will circle around me and him.

Carter turns on his barstool and locks his eyes with mine as I slowly advance toward him. With each step that I take, getting closer and closer to him, another flame ignites inside me. I don't know how I'm supposed to talk to him when there's a fire burning in me, but I'm going to have to try to ignore my body. It's going to be so hard though. I haven't been too successful in ignoring my body's desires for the past two months, and now he's actually in the same state as me, the same city as me, and the same bar as me. Damn, this is unreal. But how wrong is it that a big part of me wants to skip the conversation and just mount this man? Damn.

Carter rises off his seat, right as I stop in front of him. "You're so beautiful," he says, staring into my eyes.

The heat automatically combusts all around us and it's mixed with lustful desires. My inner vixen immediately sprawls her naked flesh out on her red, silk sheets in a very sensual way. Jesus, I want this man. My body wants this man. Fuck, I can't even think clearly.

"Thank you," I murmur, managing some words out.

"Savannah Lewis," he says smoothly. Ooh, that voice and those eyes, which haven't left mine for a second.

"Carter?" I say, giving him a questioning look.

"Bennett," he says, answering my unasked question. "Carter Bennett."

"So, Carter Bennett, where would you like to talk?"

"Can I take you to that small Mexican diner that's across the street?"

"Sure," I respond. A public place is neutral. It's safe. And hopefully, it's less tempting to do anything risqué.

Carter turns slightly and finishes his beer, and then he leaves a tip on the bar. He comes to my side and grabs my hand and threads his fingers through mine. And in that innocent connection, but one that sears our skin, we turn our heads and look at one another, our eyes instantly connecting as electric sparks are passed back and forth from his body to mine and my body to his. Whoa, it's like the last two months of my desires are crashing down on me in full force, and the loneliness quickly vanishes.

As we leave the bar, I catch Chris's eyes on Carter and I, and he's watching us impassively, but I know better than that. I know that he wishes that I was leaving with him instead. I just hope he can find someone else soon and get me out of his system.

In the hole-in-the-wall restaurant, we slide into a booth opposite of each other, the heat still circling around us. "Would you like to share some nachos?" Carter asks me.

"Yes, that sounds good." I had a tuna and egg sandwich before I left for the bar tonight, so I should probably eat something else to balance out the alcohol that I've consumed this evening.

We place our order with the waitress, and then Carter starts talking. "You're famous," he says, grinning.

"No." I shake my head. "Not even close. I just have a nice following, and Intoxication is my home on Friday nights."

"Well, from what I heard and witnessed tonight, you are well on your way."

"Were you there for both of my performances?"

"Yes," he says, staring into my eyes. "And you were completely mesmerizing. You blew me away. You have a great talent."

"Thank you," I murmur.

"I could not believe that the Savannah Lewis that the MC announced was you. I choked on my beer a little when I saw you take the stage."

"I couldn't believe my eyes when I saw you either. I pinched myself."

"After two months of," he begins, but stops as our waitress approaches. She sets down our Coronas and lets us know she'll be back shortly with our nachos.

"What were you starting to say?" I ask him.

"Oh, it was nothing really," he says, and his eyes don't give anything away as he still stares into mine. He picks up his beer. "Are you from here? Is Chicago your home?" he asks, and then he takes a drink.

Hmm, I'm curious to know what he was about to say, but I won't dwell on it. Finding out where he's from, who he is, and why he left so suddenly is what I need answered more than anything. And it seems that is where our conversation is going now.

My inner vixen wraps her red, silk sheet around herself and sits up a little in a reclined position, ready for his answers as well.

"Yes, I'm a product of the windy city," I tell him, and then I grab my beer. His eyes are burning into mine, and I clutch my beer a little firmer.

Damn, I intended to interrogate him, but his presence is overwhelming me entirely. It seems that the attraction and the pull to him are even more extreme than it was in Hawaii. Damn.

"It's kind of surreal," he says.

"What is?" I ask, as that could mean many things between us and our situation. There are lots of surreal parts to our story, even though our story was very brief and short lived.

"I've been living here in Chicago for a month now," he says. "I heard about Intoxication just from word on the street."

"It really is a small world," I state. "But from the moment we met, it's been dreamlike." I take a drink of my beer.

"I agree," he says, and then I swear I see what I think is a small bit of regret in his eyes. He takes a deep breath and exhales.

Just then, before Carter can get out and articulate whatever is going through his mind, our waitress comes back with our nachos. She sets the big plate in-between us and tells us to enjoy. Then Carter's eyes are on mine again.

"I'm so sorry, Savannah," he says, his eyes looking apologetic, and his voice sounding sincere.

My inner vixen sits up straighter, crosses her legs, and her eyes widen. Now we're getting somewhere.

"I know. You said that in your note, Carter." I pause for a few seconds and gather my thoughts before speaking them.

The only thing speaking in these hushed seconds is the intense heat that circles us. God, it speaks volumes, almost as if we don't need to exchange words. I mean, I already feel like this man knows me. That's why I stayed the night with him. But the fact is I don't know him, and he doesn't know me.

"We agreed on one night, but I probably shouldn't have stayed with you after we had sex," I say in all honesty. And before I can continue, Carter stops me.

"No," he strongly says. "I asked you to spend the entire night with me. I wanted you to."

"But then why....." I start, and he stops me again.

"I don't know," he quickly says. "I guess I freaked out," he confesses. "It had been a while since I'd been with a woman so intimately, but I was not prepared for how severely and powerfully I reacted to you, especially when I woke up with you next to me."

"So you freaked out and didn't say goodbye, but you made sure that I was supplied with breakfast." I'm pretty sure my eyes have a slightly confused look in them as I stare into his.

"Yeah, I'm an ass and a gentleman." He looks at me impassively.

"That's an interesting combination." I smile at him, and then I pick up a loaded nacho chip and begin eating.

"Indeed it is," he agrees, and picks up a nacho chip. "I truly am sorry, Savannah. I'm still trying to figure it all out."

"Thank you, but you don't need to apologize. After all, it was just a one-night stand with no strings attached." I don't need an apology from him. I just wanted to know why, and now I do, even if his answer is vague.

"You really are amazing," he says, grinning.

"And you are a mystery," I state. "But a mystery that I would like to solve," I add.

His smile widens, and he chuckles a little. "I like you, Savannah."

"I like you, too, Carter, but I would really like to know you."

He nods and doesn't waste any time. "I'm from Las Vegas, Nevada," he says. "I left there a month ago and came here. I needed a change in my life."

"Las Vegas to Chicago, that's a big change," I acknowledge.

"It is," he agrees. "But I wanted to get far away, and I've always loved Chicago, plus I know a couple people here, so I packed up my life and didn't look back."

Damn. He went to Hawaii just to get away for a day. He crashed the wedding, and then a short time later, he just picked up and moved across the country. He's spontaneous. I like that. I like that a lot.

"I like your impulsiveness." I smile at him.

He smiles back at me. "And I like your wild side," he says, remembering our fun that we had in the ocean I'm sure.

"I think spontaneity and wild go great together." I take a drink of my beer, and then pick up a loaded nacho chip. "And I think we proved that in Hawaii," I add, and then bite into my chip.

"I can't argue that," he says, and picks up another loaded nacho chip.

We eat the nachos in silence for the next few minutes, but it's a charged silence, as we hold each other's gaze and the heat continues to envelop us.

"Savannah Lewis, the sexy, beautiful, talented poetess and writer," he says, grinning.

I smile, and then pick up my beer and take a drink.

"So you write erotic poetry, and you have books published, so you write stories as well," he says. "Are your stories erotic, too?" he asks me.

I smile brighter. He really was watching me as he waited for me at the bar while I conversed with my fans. "They're erotic and romantic."

"How many books do you have published?"

"Ten," I reply. "They are short stories, and I'm currently writing my first full-length novel."

"That's incredible. You should be very proud of yourself."

"Thank you." I am proud of my accomplishments, but I don't voice it. I'm humble and very grateful.

"Are your parents proud of your work?" he asks. "I remember how they were with each other on the dance floor in Hawaii. I assume you come from a very open and entertaining family."

I giggle. He glimpsed a small sliver of what my parents are like. He really has no idea at all. "They are very proud. They sell my books in their store."

"Really," he says, and picks up his beer. "So, they own a bookstore?" He takes a drink.

"No." I shake my head and giggle a little. "Not even close. You see, sex has always been an everyday word in my house. It's been in my vocabulary ever since I could put a sentence together." I pause for a second. Just having the word sex come out of my mouth in Carter's presence right now is igniting more flames inside me. I take in a breath through my nose, trying to be discreet, and let it out. "My parents own an erotic store that sells sex toys, lingerie, and steamy books. It's called Ooh, Erotic Pleasures."

"Wow," he voices. "That's really cool."

"It is," I agree.

"Savannah, you are a very interesting and intriguing woman. I definitely want to know more about you."

"Ditto," I say.

"Can I take you out tomorrow, maybe dinner?"

"Sure, that sounds nice." I smile.

"I'd like to make sure you get home safely," he offers. "Do we need a cab? Do you live far?"

"I'm just five blocks away, so if you'd like to walk, we can."

"It's a beautiful night. A walk would be pleasant." He smiles at me.

Yeah, and it's better than being confined in the back of a cab with him and our heat. It's bound to explode if I'm enclosed in a space with him. And although I want him and my body wants him, I don't know if we're ready for that just yet.

We finish up our nachos and drink the rest of our beer. Carter pays the tab, and we exit the diner.

He takes my hand in his and threads his fingers through mine as we walk the streets of Chicago and feel the warm night air on us. The heat follows us, and the electric energy continues to pass from his body to mine and my body to his. Damn. Maybe another night together is what we need to tame the fire between us.

Our conversation along the way is casual, just talking about Chicago and what we love about the city. It's nice, and it flows until we reach my door.

"You're so beautiful," he says, caressing my cheek, lighting up my skin and insides even more than they already are.

My keys are in my hand, ready to unlock my door. But his eyes are hypnotic, and his touch is blistering. I'm frozen by him.

He presses his lips to mine, and I instantly begin dripping into my panties. He wraps his arms around my waist at the same time that I wrap my hands around his neck, and then our tongues meet and taste and twirl with each other as his hands are at the small of my back and pressing me into him. I feel his desire. I taste his desire. It matches mine. No more maybes. We need another night.

After a red-hot minute, Carter pulls his lips off mine, and we're both breathing hard. We stare into each other's eyes as we try to control our breathing, and then he speaks. "I've been fighting the urge to be with you again," he admits.

"Don't fight it. Stay with me," I tell him.

A seductive groan escapes through his mouth, and then he presses his lips to mine again.

Chapter Nine

We stumble into my apartment, in each other's arms as our kiss consumes us with passion. Carter kicks the door shut, and I swear it just got twenty degrees hotter in here.

"Lead the way, Savannah," he says, pulling his lips off mine, his breathing labored, his voice a little rough. "Because I'm ready to rip your clothes off and take you right here, but I would prefer to go slow and take my time with you."

Damn. That's really fucking hot, but I would prefer my bedroom as well. For the amount of passion and heat being passed back and forth between us and claiming us, we definitely need a bed. I take his hand and take him to my room.

Carter is behind me as I'm closing my door. His hands are on my waist, his fingers inching into my skirt, and he's nuzzling my neck as his erection presses into me. I'm dripping nonstop into my panties. My body is lit up all over, inside and out. And I just might explode before he even enters me.

He begins pulling down my red pencil skirt, and then his hands are on my backside, gripping my cheeks over and over. It's a vigorous caress on my ass, and I start moaning.

"That's a hot sound coming out of your mouth," he murmurs at my ear. "You like this," he inquires, his hands still squeezing my cheeks repeatedly.

"Yes," I breathe. "I love attention on and in my ass."

I feel his erection get bigger and harder at my admission, and he swallows hard. "Damn, you wild woman," he murmurs, and then he pulls my skirt down the rest of the way. "Turn around," he tells me, and I do.

I lock my eyes on his and pull my red belly shirt over my head, dropping it on the floor. He places his hands on my backside once again and resumes his vigorous caress, pulling me into his hard, muscular frame. My lips part as the moaning is at the tip of my tongue, but I bite my bottom lip and suppress my vocals.

"You are so gorgeous," he says, holding my eyes with his.

I place my fingers at the hem of his blue Guess t-shirt, just melting into his hands, wearing only my white satin bra and matching thong, plus my white open-toe heels. Then I start lifting his t-shirt up, and he helps me, removing his hands from my ass, but then gripping my cheeks even harder again as his shirt falls to the floor.

"Oh god, you're gorgeous, too," I say as I place my hands on his sick-pack and run them up his chest. My visions of him in my dreams and waking thoughts are hot, but the real man at the tip of my fingers is so much better, so much hotter.

I grip his biceps and place my lips on his, kissing him softly, but he immediately deepens the kiss, and I begin moaning all over his tongue.

I'm dripping and dripping, and my panties are so soiled now that they can't hold anymore of my arousal. I can feel it slowly escaping from the thin satin and oozing down my thighs. My entire pussy is throbbing, my clit and my lips, all of it, inside and out. I'm definitely going to explode before his cock enters me.

Hmm, his cock, it's gorgeous, too, but let me remind myself. I move my hands down to his jeans and make quick work of unbuttoning and unzipping them. Then I reach inside his boxer briefs and grab his big, hard cock. He moans into my mouth, and then I grab his balls and squeeze them. He moans again, squeezes my ass a bit harder, and that has me moaning louder all over his tongue.

Carter groans and breaks our kiss. "Get on the bed," he tells me, his voice rough and his breathing ragged.

Wow! He's much different from our night in Hawaii. On the island, even though he wanted me just as much as I wanted him, he seemed less assured with everything that was happening between us. But now, he's completely confident and taking total charge. It's really hot.

Before I follow instructions, I squeeze the tip of his cock, getting his pre-cum between my forefinger and thumb. He gasps, and I bring my thumb and finger to my mouth and taste a piece of him. I moan at his yummy flavor, and he watches me, breathing so very ragged.

He growls a moan and squeezes my ass really hard. Then I lick his lips and kiss him softly. He smirks at me in a sexy way, his eyes turning a darker shade of blue. Then he smacks my backside.

"Ooh... Do that again," I insist. I really like his hands on my ass, squeezing and smacking, it all feels so good.

He smacks my backside once more, and then he says, "Your bed is waiting for us."

Oh, it definitely is. Damn right! I smile at him, and then I walk to my bed, pull my blue-green comforter down and climb onto my white cotton sheets. I lie against a pillow as Carter steps to the foot of my bed.

He takes off his shoes and socks, and then he begins taking off his jeans and boxer briefs, his eyes on me the whole time. "You know," he says after a silent but heated minute, "I was undressing you with my eyes while you were on stage reciting your poetry." He grabs my ankles, wrapping his hands around them, and he pulls me down along the bed, so that I'm flat on my back.

I gasp and squeal at his strong and quick actions, but keep my eyes on his.

"Both poems," he adds, and he begins taking my heels off. Then he drops them on the floor. "The real you, the unclothed you," he says, climbing onto the bed and on top of me, "is absolutely breathtaking." He swallows hard as he crawls up my body.

Oh damn, my panties are soaked, in-between my thighs are wet, and I can feel a small wet spot forming on the sheets. My clit is throbbing and throbbing and throbbing. I'm so close to exploding, and he hasn't even done anything to me yet.

My inner vixen, who sprawled herself back onto her red, silk sheets the moment Carter kissed me outside of my apartment door, is already touching herself and panting hard.

"You're gorgeous," he says, staring down into my eyes, covering my body with his like a warm blanket, a sexy, heated blanket. "Every single inch of you," he adds.

I bite my bottom lip, a sexy whimper sounding through, and drip out of my panties, in-between my thighs some more, and onto the sheets some more, too. His eyes are fierce and glowing a really dark blue, and I'm lost in them more than I've ever been.

Carter brings his thumb to my bottom lip, caresses it, and then gently pulls it free. "That's a sexy look on you," he says, then kisses me. It's a juicy kiss. His cock rubs against my sex, and I squeeze my thighs against him as I grind into him. But then he quickly breaks the kiss. "You're so wet," he hoarsely states, his cock pulsating against my panties.

"I'm so aroused. I'm spilling out of my panties. It's all in-between my thighs and getting all over the sheets. It's what you do to me, Carter. My orgasm is just one more touch, one more kiss away."

"Oh, Savannah, I'm going to have you coming repeatedly then, because I want every single curve of your body ingrained into my memory." He unhooks the clasp at the front of my bra and releases my breasts.

"Oh shit," I breathe. He's going to own me by the end of the night. After all, he's the first man to give me an orgasm without my added aid or coaxing it along.

"So nice," he says, hooking his fingers into my thong and gradually pulling it down my legs. "You've made an intoxicating aroma, and your pussy is glimmering with your thick arousal all over it and all around it."

I flash him a sensual smile and give him a wink, too. The delicious smell of sex is filling my room, and we're just getting started.

Carter rises on his knees and holds up my thong. "It's completely and utterly drenched and still dripping. This is what I do to you?"

I nod and bite my bottom lip.

He drops my thong on the bed and grabs his cock. He squeezes the tip and gets a nice, thick amount of pre-cum between his forefinger and thumb, and it's actually a lot for just pre-cum. Then he hovers over me and brings his sticky arousal to my lips. "And this is what you do to me," he says, and I open my mouth and suck him clean. And a low but deep growl escapes his lips as he watches me.

"Fuck me, Carter. Make me come over and over," I urge as soon as he removes his finger and thumb from my mouth.

"I'm taking my time with you," he says, his eyes heated but serious. Then he presses his lips to mine.

This kiss is unhurried, yet it's calculated and packed with extreme passion. His lips are strong, moving mine like a command, and yet they're soft, too, like a sweet caress. Our tongues slow dance against each other and our bodies begin to rock together. He cups my face in his hands and devours my mouth a little harder. And that's it. This kiss is my undoing.

I grip his biceps, moaning all over our kiss. His cock presses against my sex, and I release my first orgasm in-between our scorching flesh.

Carter pulls his lips off mine, just pulling back an inch, still holding my face in his hands, and stares down into my eyes. "Let me hear you," he says, and rocks his cock against my sex a little harder.

I moan loudly and spill out the rest of my orgasm, my legs slightly shaking against his body.

"Beautiful," he says, and kisses my lips softly, unmoving his position on me. "Perfect," he adds, and kisses me softly again.

"Carter," I breathe, and another wave of pleasure runs through my body, and I grip him tighter as I quiver.

"Watching you come undone beneath me is the sexiest thing I've ever witnessed, and I want to witness it again and again." He releases my face, placing one hand at my nape. Then he moves his other hand to my backside and grips it firmly.

"Oh...." I moan as he very slowly trails his nose along my neck, connecting with my skin and deeply inhaling.

He trails his nose from my ear down to my shoulder and keeps going along the length of my arm, inhaling every step of the way. It's different. It's new to me. But it's so hot. It's making my pussy drip all over again.

He removes his hand from my nape, places it on my other ass cheek, and grips it firmly. Then he very slowly trails his nose along the other side of my neck. He inhales down to my shoulder and continues down the length of my arm. And I drip onto the sheets some more.

"Oh...." I moan.

Carter pauses for a minute, staring into my eyes, and squeezes my backside repeatedly.

"Oh.... Oh.... Oh...." I moan and moan and moan.

He brings his face to mine, like he's going to kiss me, but he doesn't. Instead, he runs his nose along my slightly parted lips and inhales. Then he pulls back and gazes at me.

"You're a rare and beautiful gem, Savannah." He squeezes my ass cheeks, and then drops his head to the top of my breasts and deeply inhales. He squeezes my backside again and inhales again, too.

"Oh...." I moan. "Carter," I breathe.

He slowly trails his nose around one breast, at my nipple, at my areola, and all over the rest of it. He buries his nose all over and around it, inhaling constantly. Then his nose is trailing my other breast in the same exact way. And I'm a dripping wet mess.

God, he's like an animal, and I have the scent that he so desperately desires.

He releases my backside and moves down my body, slowly trailing his nose all over my belly and inhaling. He's so close to my sex that I begin breathing harder, and my clit swells in anticipation. But that's not where his nose takes him.

Damn!

I want to tell him to go back to my pussy and unleash his animalistic tendencies there, but he's successfully seducing me. And it feels amazing to be at the receiving end of persuasion. It's not something that I'm really used to, but I could totally see myself getting very used to it with this man.

He grabs my leg, lifting it off the bed, and he very slowly trails his nose along my thigh and all the way down my leg, deeply inhaling, until he reaches my foot. Then he locks his eyes on mine and gradually licks the instep of my foot. And a wave of pleasure shoots straight to my core, causing my clit to throb with another hot buildup of juice wanting to pour out and saturate my bed some more.

I stare into his dark sapphires, panting, and loosely grab the sheets in my hands.

He lays my leg down and lifts up my other leg. But this time, he licks the instep of my foot first, and he holds my gaze as he does. And another wave of pleasure rocks my core, causing my body to faintly quiver.

"Oh, Carter.... I'm.... I'm...." Oh god, I'm so close. But before I can form anymore words, he's slowly trailing his nose up my leg, connecting to my skin and deeply inhaling.

He pauses at my sex, and I grip the sheets, panting and watching him. "She is so beautiful," he says, staring at my glistening folds and my throbbing clit. "So beautiful," he repeats, and then deeply inhales, very deeply.

My entire body quivers.

He carefully yet obsessively moves his nose through my dripping wet folds and up to my clit, rubbing on my clit, and inhaling my pussy juices. And that's it. This carnal need for my scent is my undoing.

I grip the sheets harder, moaning loudly, and sink into them a little more as I release my second orgasm very close to his watching eyes.

"So beautiful and so responsive," he murmurs, and then begins kissing my vibrating thighs, one, and then the other.

And just when I think he's finally going to give my pussy his undivided attention, he starts moving back up my body, kissing my heated flesh all over. And his tender, wet kisses sizzle on my skin.

"Every," he whispers, and kisses my breast. "Curve," he whispers, and kisses my other breast. "Ingrained," he whispers, and kisses my neck. "Into my," he whispers, and kisses the other side of my neck. "Memory," he whispers, staring down into my eyes.

I quietly whimper and stare right back into his, ready to come apart underneath him again, from another kiss, from another touch, I'm so ready.

He presses his lips to mine, silencing my sexual whimpers. He presses his body into mine, too, and his cock presses onto my swollen, sexually sensitive clit. And that's it. This man is my undoing.

I move my hands around his neck and into his hair, and I wrap my legs around him and gently grind my sex into him as my third orgasm flows out of me.

And Carter kisses me until my body relaxes in his arms.

"The sheets are so wet," I murmur, feeling the massive puddles as I lie in it all.

"Not wet enough," he says, and then he moves down my body until his face is at my sex.

Oh yes! Lick me.

He places his thumbs on my wet folds and easily opens me up. Then he deeply inhales. "So good," he murmurs, and then he very slowly runs his tongue in-between my wet opening. And he's looking up into my eyes as he does.

"Oh shit," I breathe.

"Damn, you taste good, too," he murmurs, and then he licks through my opening again. And right after that, a low growl rumbles in his chest. "You have the best flavor," he adds, and he licks through once again.

Oh my god! His tongue, I really like his tongue.

I place my hands in Carter's hair, and I watch him eat me out. I watch his eyes afire as they drink in my pussy and drink in my hot and bothered body and drink in my glazed over, euphoric eyes. I watch his thumbs hold me in place. I watch his tongue lick through my sex up to my clit, over and over. I move my fingers through his hair, and I watch him.

And then suddenly, he gets a little more aggressive and really starts giving my pussy his undivided attention. He literally devours my entire sex like a starved animal, sucking on my lips, sucking on my clit, and sucking my juices. And he's relentless.

I'm panting and moaning simultaneously. I'm continuously kneading his head, almost fisting his hair. And I'm still watching him. My orgasm is close, so close.

And as if his savage actions aren't enough, he begins quietly growling moans as he hungrily feasts on me. And that's it. That does it. His hot noises, his tongue, his whole mouth is my undoing.

My legs start shaking, and I fist chunks of his hair and throw my head back as my fourth orgasm spills out of me. I ride immense waves of pleasure as Carter's mouth fills with my warm liquid.

"Oh, Carter," I breathe.

He grabs my hands and takes them out of his hair. He threads his fingers through mine and places our entwined hands above my head as he moves up my body. Then he presses his lips to mine and kisses me deeply and ardently.

The head of his big, hard cock is pushing inside my sex, and my inner walls are already trying to latch on.

Carter pulls his lips off mine. "She wants this dick," he says, staring down into my eyes. "And my dick wants her, wants you," he says, and then pushes his cock the rest of the way inside me.

And we both gasp as he occupies and fills me entirely.

"Oh, Savannah, you are so tight. You feel so good." He squeezes my hands above my head, not letting go.

My body is completely open to him, and my inner walls are hugging him. I bring my legs up, bending them, and I spread them open just a little more. And I get lost in his possession of me.

He hasn't even begun to move inside me yet, and I'm already anticipating an orgasm. It's not far out of my reach. I can feel it building in me, and the feeling gets more intense by the second as his eyes own mine.

And just as he begins to pull back and start to move, he pulls out all the way to the tip of his cock. Then he slowly pushes it back inside, and we both gasp again as my inner walls welcome him.

He fills me deep and stills. Then he does it all over again. He pulls his cock out, leaving the tip inside me, and then he pushes it back in. We both gasp as my walls hug him again, and then he stills once again.

"Come for me, Savannah," he says, and then he pulls his cock out to the tip all over again. And this is the pace he has set. He continues to stare into my eyes, squeeze my hands, push his cock all the way inside me, and pulling it back out again, over and over.

I'm softly panting, but my orgasm is fast approaching. And it's evident in his eyes as well. He's close, too.

He pulls back and thrusts into me hard. And that's it. This man, his cock, is making me come. He's making himself come, too.

"Ah!" I cry out as my fifth orgasm rushes out of me, my body quivering beneath him. And he's buried in me so deep, my cream drips down to his balls.

And Carter loudly grunts and spills his nut inside me at the same time that my thick juices begin coating his balls.

And the penetration of my sex is just getting started.

He releases my hands and wraps his arms around me, circling me in his blistering embrace. He presses his lips to mine, and I wrap my entire body around him as he slowly pushes his tongue in my mouth. Then he starts to thrust in me, nice and slow, as our mouths make hot love.

I'm moaning on his lips, on his tongue, and all in his mouth. And he's quietly moaning, too.

My walls are glued to him. My pussy is swallowing him.

His cock is throbbing deep. His cock is swelling harder.

Damn. His cock feels so fucking good. He feels so good. Shit, everything he has done to me tonight has felt so good. I'm lost in ecstasy. I've been lost in it ever since his lips touched mine outside my apartment door.

I hear the ecstasy. I taste the ecstasy. I feel the ecstasy. It's filling my bedroom. It's circling us. It's dominating us. It's consuming us. The ecstasy is him. The ecstasy is me. The ecstasy is us.

He thrusts in me, filling me deep each and every time. And we both find our orgasms, reaching them in unison.

We break our hot lip connection, both of our bodies shaking in one another's arms, and we shout each other's names, gripping each other tightly.

Neither one of us make any attempts to move. We just hold each other and stare into each other's eyes as we softly pant.

But he's the first to speak. "I think the sheets are wet enough now."

"I think they've soaked through to the mattress."

He smiles at me. "I think you're right." He kisses my lips tenderly. "You're amazing," he says, and then kisses me again.

"So are you." A small yawn escapes my mouth.

My inner vixen, who had a wild and wet time right along with me, has already got her sheets twisted around her, and she's succumbed to sleep.

"I don't think I can move," I murmur as my eyes get heavy. And all I can think is that this man owns me completely. He's left his mark on me again, but this time is so much more profound.

"You don't have to," he says, and rolls us over, so that he's on his back, and we're out of the huge puddles that form one enormous wet spot.

He kisses my forehead. The moon peeks through my slightly open blinds, as it has been all evening. And I fall asleep in his arms, warm and sated.

Chapter Ten

I hear birds chirping outside my bedroom window, and I begin to open my eyes. The sun is shining through my blinds, and it looks like a beautiful Saturday morning.

I stretch out in my bed, and then all the hot events that took place last night instantly flood my mind. Carter, his kisses, his hands, his nose, his tongue, his cock, damn, I've never had that many orgasms in one night.

Carter.

But he's not in my bed. Shit! Not again.

I immediately jump out of bed and rip the sheets off. They are soiled from my many orgasms and from our perspiration, plus they smell like him. They really smell like him. And if he's going to play these types of games with me, then I can't have any extra reminders of him. I already have memories and those damn dreams that won't go away.

I didn't have any dreams while I slept in his arms though, but I'm sure they will return and plague my nights now.

I grab a long t-shirt out of my dresser drawer and slip it on. Then I gather the sheets and walk out of my bedroom. And I'm automatically curious. I hear someone moving around in the kitchen, and it sounds like they are rummaging through the pots and pans. But Lacy doesn't cook much, especially breakfast, plus she stayed out last night with Brian. And Abby spent the night with Steve, so I don't think she would be home yet either. So, who's in my kitchen?

Hmm, I drop the sheets and go find out.

"Good morning, Savannah," Carter greets me with a smile.

He's here. He's still here. Any frustration that I was feeling starts to gradually fade away.

Damn, he looks good, too. He's fresh and clean, showered no doubt while I was still sleeping.

"Good morning." I smile. "You cook?" I ask him.

"Sometimes, yes," he says. "And I would like to cook you breakfast."

"I thought you left," I admit.

"I wouldn't do that to you again, Savannah. I regret that I've already done it to you once."

"So...." I pause on the word. I'm not sure what other words I'm searching for.

"So I had the best time with you last night, and I would like to have some great times with you during the day, too."

"Like dating me," I inquire.

"Yes." He grins.

"Okay." I smile brighter.

He takes a few steps and stops right in front of me. Then he takes my face in his hands and gazes into my eyes. "I'm not going anywhere, unless you want me to," he says, and then kisses me.

"So breakfast," I say, and smile at him.

He releases my face, grinning. "Yes," he says. "Why don't you go freshen up, and I'll have breakfast ready when you're finished."

"Okay." I turn on my heel and walk back to the hallway and pick up my sheets. Then I throw them in the washing machine with some of my other laundry as I'm on my way to the bathroom.

I take a look in the mirror, and I can't help but beam at myself. It's amazing how everything can change so quickly in a day. The mystery man wants to date me. And even though both of us would like to know each other better, I did not expect this, but I'm very curious to see how things develop from here and where our undeniable attraction leads us.

But the one thing that I do know for sure is that the sex will be mind-blowing fireworks. It already is.

I spend the next fifteen minutes or so freshening up, brushing my teeth and showering. Then I slip on a clean thong and bra, a pink t-shirt, and light blue cotton shorts, and return to the kitchen.

"You're right on-time," Carter says, turning off one of the burners on the stove.

"Wow, you have been busy." I grab a couple plates out of the cupboard, along with two glasses, and then two forks out of the silverware drawer. I set the table, and Carter brings the food over.

"This is the breakfast we would've had if I hadn't of freaked out and left," he says, pulling out the chair for me to sit.

He has made pancakes, scrambled eggs, and bacon, plus he cut up the rest of the strawberries that I had in the fridge, and he made tea.

I take a seat, and Carter scoots me in a little. He picks up our glasses and fills them with ice water, and then he takes a seat across from me.

"This is wonderful." I smile at him. "Thank you."

"It's my pleasure." He grins. "Is water and tea okay? I couldn't find any coffee."

"Yeah, we keep forgetting to buy it, and now I'm getting kind of used to not having it." I start placing food on my plate.

"Who's we?" he asks, and starts filling his plate, too.

"Oh, that would be my sister, Lacy, and my best friend, Abby. They live here, too, but they're not here most mornings anymore. They both have new men in their lives, and their minds are preoccupied."

"New love has a tendency to do that," he says, and begins cutting up his pancakes. And I briefly wonder if Lacy is really falling in love. I know Abby is, but Lacy doesn't fall in love too easily. Plus, she just met Brian, but they already do look very smitten with one another, so it's possible.

"Yeah," I agree, and pick up a piece of bacon. "So, what do you do, Carter?" I bite into my bacon.

"Well, for several years, I worked at the MGM Grand in Vegas. I was a manger in the casino."

"That sounds cool."

"It was for the most part, but it's not what I was born to do I guess you could say."

"And what is it you're born to do?"

"I'm an artist," he says. "I sketch, and I draw, but I love to paint more than anything. That's where my heart is."

Oh wow. We're both artists, me with words, and him with the stroke of a paintbrush. I paint a story with sexy, intriguing words, and he literally paints the story on a canvas as he sees it. Damn, are we kindred spirits? Because it feels more and more like we are with each piece of information that surfaces.

We continue to eat and dive further into the conversation.

"I began to get really tired of wasting my time doing something that I wasn't passionate about," he explains. "And that's what it felt like, like I was wasting all my time, but more like I was wasting my talent."

"So, then you moved here?"

"Yes. I woke up one morning and decided that I wasn't going to be stuck anymore. I decided that I was going to take the risk and follow my heart and chase my dream. And a bigger city seemed like the best place to be."

"And since you've always loved Chicago and know a couple people here," I say, because I pay attention to every word that comes out of his mouth.

"Exactly," he says. "I didn't even have to think twice about it."

"I admire anyone that just goes for it. Life is too short to be unhappy."

"That is the truth," he agrees, and takes a drink of his tea.

"So, have you been painting nonstop since you moved here?" I pick up my tea and take a sip, and then I place a strawberry in my mouth.

"I have." He grins, and so do his eyes. "And I bought a building. That's the first thing I did when I arrived in this city."

"A building," I question.

"Yes, for my gallery."

"You have a gallery." My eyes widen in surprise. It's incredible. That's a big deal.

"Yes, it opened two weeks ago, and it was highlighted in all the local papers."

Wow! I probably would've known that if I read any of the newspapers, but I'm always too focused on my writing, and I'd rather read a good book instead of the news. It's usually always depressing anyways.

"That's quick. You've only been here for a month."

"Well, I did a little research a few days before I moved, and I made a few phone calls and arranged to look at a few buildings as soon as I got here. And the second building I looked at and walked through was perfect, so I purchased it and started getting it ready for my artwork immediately."

"That's amazing." I smile at him, and he returns my smile.

"Yeah, I was lucky to have the couple people that I know here give me a lot of their time and help." He picks up a piece of bacon. "I know a total of three people in this city, my brother, Caleb, his wife, Ashley, and you."

Damn, I feel like I'm blushing, which is so not like me. He has a list, and I'm on it. My inner vixen looks up from her engrossing book and smiles from ear to ear, matching precisely how I'm feeling.

"What are your drawings and paintings like? Do you only stick to a certain theme?"

"I draw and paint whatever I find beauty in," he says. "I experience something. I see something. I witness something, and I create my art from my memories."

"Wow, that's impressive. You're a complete natural."

"Just like you," he says. "You create art from the world around you, too."

"I do," I agree. "I take from experiences, things I've seen, things I've read, and places I've been."

"It seems we have a lot more in common than just two people who are good at being alone."

"Yeah," I agree, and smile warmly.

We eat in silence for a few minutes, a comfortable silence, yet with a little heat surrounding us, but it's not blazing flames at the moment. I think we sort of extinguished the hot coals for now, or maybe we just wore it out. Although, the longer we sit here staring intently at each other, the more and more I feel the heat building and rising between us.

"I would still like to take you out to dinner tonight," he says, our breakfast just about finished. "And after that, I want to have some fun with you," he adds.

"Some sexy fun," I state, "or some dirty fun."

He chuckles a little. "I really like how your mind operates, but I'd say both sexy and dirty."

"I like that you like how my mind works, and I like where your mind is going, too. Sexy and dirty is a very intriguing combination. I'll handle the dirty part."

He chuckles more now and a bit louder. "I bet you will."

A couple more bites and we're done with our food. Then I walk Carter to the door. I have more chapters to write, and he has some work to do as well.

"I'll pick you up at eight," he tells me, and then he cups my chin and kisses me tenderly, but lingers there for a minute. He releases me right as the heat produces a flame. "See you soon, Savannah."

"Bye, Carter." And he's out the door, me closing and locking it behind him.

I go back to the kitchen and clean up all of the dishes, and then I sit down with my laptop and pick up where I left off at, writing my sexy novel.

*   *   *   *   *   *   *   *

"I can't be the man I want to be without you by my side." I'm writing an intense scene, full of so much emotion, when Abby walks in the door.

"Hey, Savannah," she says, closing the door behind her as she enters. She sets her small bag down and goes to the fridge and takes out an apple.

"Hey," I say, saving my work, and then looking up from my laptop.

She sits down across from me. "How was your night?" she asks, lifting an eyebrow. Then she bites into her apple.

"It was absolutely amazing." I smile big and bright. "I've never had that many orgasms in one night."

"You had sex with him again?" Her eyes get big in their sockets.

I nod. "Yeah, he just left here a couple hours ago."

And before either one of us can say anything else, Lacy walks in the door. "Who just left here not that long ago?" she says, closing the door behind her and dropping her bag on the floor.

"Carter did," Abby says, "Carter from Hawaii."

"What? Seriously," Lacy says, and rather loudly, and then she sits down at the table with us.

"Yeah, he moved here a month ago, and he was at Intoxication last night," I explain.

"Okay, Little Vixen, spill it," Lacy says.

"Yeah," Abby agrees, "and don't leave anything out."

I push my laptop aside, and I start talking. "Okay, as soon as I spoke the last words of my poetry from my second performance last night, I saw him emerge from the crowd." I start from the very beginning and tell Abby and Lacy everything from that point of the night up until he walked out the door this morning, and I give them enough details, just not every single one.

"Damn," Lacy says, "I can't wait to meet this guy."

"Yeah," Abby agrees, nodding and smiling.

"I'm happy for you," Lacy says, smiling at me.

"Yeah, Savannah, this is a wonderful turn of events," Abby says, still smiling.

"It really is," I agree. "We have easy conversations, incredible, amazing sex, and we are discovering that we have quite a bit in common." I smile, an all teeth smile at them both.

"When are you seeing him again?" Lacy asks me.

"He's picking me up tonight and taking me to dinner, and then he said he wants to have some fun with me after that."

"Cool," Lacy says, and rises from her seat. "I've got to get ready for work. Mom and Dad are waiting for me. Dad's trying to take Mom out on Lake Michigan to go paddle boarding, stand up paddle boarding."

"Oh, that will be fun."

Lacy nods, and then she heads to the bathroom.

"I'm going to get out of here, too," Abby says, rising from her seat as well. She walks to the garbage can and throws away her apple core. "I'm going grocery shopping," she tells me.

"Oh cool," I say, scooting my laptop back in front of me. "Don't forget the coffee," I mention.

"I'll try not to." She grabs her wallet out of her small bag and takes her keys out of her pocket. "I'll see you in a little while." She walks to the door.

"Bye," I call, and then she waves, and she's gone.

I get back to my book and begin writing, completely focused on my characters and their story. And twenty minutes later, Lacy, who is now in her bedroom after a quick shower, is walking out of her room and to the door.

"Bye, Little Vixen," she says, waving. "Have fun tonight."

"I will." I smile. "Bye." And she's gone.

Without anymore distractions, I stare at the computer screen as my fingers fill it with word after word. And I don't move an inch until it's time for me to get ready for my date.

*　　　*　　　*　　　*　　　*　　　*　　　*　　　*

"Dinner was excellent, Carter. Thank you."

We've just left Shelly's Oyster Shack. It's a seafood restaurant that's located off the shores of Lake Michigan. They have several ways to prepare oysters, plus they prepare a huge selection of other seafood as well.

"You're welcome, Savannah." He grins and takes my hand, threading his fingers through mine, as we step out into the busy nightlife of this lively city. Then he leans in close and whispers in my ear, "I enjoyed watching you swallow those oysters." His low but deep voice and his warm breath at my ear send a spicy tingle throughout my entire body. It makes both my clit and my pussy lips hum with lust.

Damn!

But yeah, I liked watching him swallow them, too.

We shared a big plate of Oysters Rockefeller before we had our main course, him having an Oyster Po' Boy and me having the mixed seafood salad. We sat next to a big, open window that allowed us to appreciate the water and the gentle, warm breeze that touched us. We had great conversations about our college days and our family life. It was nice, easy, and it all felt so natural with him, plus everything was very delicious.

Now my belly is full, and Carter is becoming less and less of a mystery with each exchange of dialogue that we have. I feel our connection getting deeper.

We're walking along the Lakefront Trail of Lake Michigan, and it's a beautiful night. The moon is brightly glowing over the water, silhouetting the waves as they rise and fall.

Carter and I are dressed nice but casual. He has on jeans, a blue button-down collar shirt that magnifies his eyes, and he has a pair of dark blue suede lace-up brogue shoes on his feet. He smells seductive, a woodsy and musky scent that's mixed with a hint of pepper. It makes me want to trail my nose all over him. And he has a day worth of scruff on his face that I'd love to feel against my wet folds. He looks very, very sexy, and I kind of want to get to the dirty part of our night right now. As it is, every fiber in my body is already craving this man and his abilities, plus I have something risqué in mind.

But he wants to have fun with me first, and I'm always down for a good time, plus I'm curious as to what he has in mind, so I'll suppress my sexual wants until later.

I'm wearing a pair of dark blue three quarter length skinny jeans, a thin white cotton cold shoulder top that clings to my breasts, and pearls beading white sandals on my feet with a light pink polish on my toes. I have tiny white gold hoops in my ears, and my hair is pulled up in a neat ponytail. I gave my eyes a subtle smoky look and my lips a light gloss. And Carter's eyes have been drinking me in all evening, so I know it's going to be another explosive night. I'm counting on it.

"How does music, alcohol, and singing sound?" Carter asks me as we are approaching a bar that's in the shape of a boat.

"Singing," I state with a questioning tone in my voice, but there's a smile on my face, because this bar looks so cool. It's a big boat, but it's not in the water. It's actually a real bar.

He nods. "It's a karaoke bar."

"Oh cool." My smile widens. I briefly heard about this place from my dad, but he failed to mention that the bar is in the shape of a boat.

"It's a new bar. Have you been here before?"

"No." I shake my head. "But it sounds really fun."

"Do you sing?" He releases my hand and opens the door for me to enter first.

"Not really," I reply, and enter the bar.

Carter is right behind me. "Me either," he says close to my ear, his warm breath tickling my neck.

"Then this should be really fun." I begin to giggle a little.

Carter smiles at me, and then leads me to a table in the middle of the bar, and it looks like a regular karaoke bar on the inside. There's a stage, a lot of people, drinks flowing, and a young man performing Baby Got Back by Sir Mix-A-Lot. It's hilarious, and it's very animated. The entire bar is very lively as well. We're definitely going to have fun.

A waitress takes our drink order and leaves us with a karaoke menu, an ongoing list of songs.

"Wow. There's so much to choose from," I say, flipping through the pages. The menu has songs from every genre of music, plus from every decade going back to the fifties.

"Yeah, they've got everything," he agrees. "Do you want to sing a couple songs together?" he asks, looking up from his menu.

I smile at him, my whole face lighting up. "Absolutely," I say. That will be hilarious.

We both write down our song choices on the small index card provided. We pick out a couple individual songs and a couple to sing together, too. Then the waitress comes back to our table with our drinks. She sets down a Rum and Coke for Carter and a Vodka Cranberry for me, plus two glasses of water. Then she takes our small song list and leaves our table.

The drinks are strong, but really good, and this place doesn't have one dull moment at all. The songs keep coming, one after the other, and there's continuously one, two, or a group of people on the stage attempting to sound like the artists from the tracks. And every few songs or so, there's actually someone that can carry a tune. It's pretty cool, and the rest of the efforts are hysterical.

Carter and I are drinking, whispering to each other, and laughing. We're having a great time. And now it's my turn, so I take the stage.

I have the Mic in my hand, my eyes on Carter, and the music begins playing. I'm singing Like a Virgin by Madonna. I get really into it, touching my body and dancing around. And whether Carter realizes or not, I'm singing it to him, because he makes me feel shiny and new, just like the song says.

I'm not as good as when I recite my poetry, but I'm not bad by any means, and I get whistles, smiles, and applause. And Carter is wearing a big smile as I take my seat at the table with him.

"You were great," he says, still grinning. "I liked your moves," he adds.

I smile and giggle. "It was really fun."

The stage gets taken over by rock moves next. Two guys get a little rambunctious as they sing Pour Some Sugar on Me by Def Leppard, and most of the crowd rocks out with them as well as us.

Then Carter gets on stage. He mellows it out a bit as he sings Losing My Religion by R. E. M. He seems to get captured by the song. Maybe the words hold some truth for him. I'm not sure, but the mystery of him is showing again. I see it in his eyes each time they briefly connect with mine.

And he's not half bad himself. He gets some applause as he comes back to our table.

"You were good," I tell him, and smile. "But don't worry, you haven't said too much."

"And not nearly enough," he murmurs, looking into my eyes.

"The mystery of Carter Bennett," I state, and then finish my drink.

He smirks like a slight grin, and then the waitress comes by with fresh drinks, setting them in front of us. She takes our empty glasses and leaves us to the fun and funny entertainment.

And the next song has me bouncing in my seat and quietly singing along, as three girls do a decent job with No Scrubs by TLC. They're not spectacular, but they own the stage, and they get the crowd dancing in their seats, not just me. Carter is tapping his foot to the beat, too.

The next several songs are more great mixtures of different genres and different decades of music. The performances are good, some much better than others, but they are all entertaining in one way or the other. Carter and I continue to enjoy our drinks, our atmosphere, and each other's company.

Carter grabs my hand. "We're on," he says. "Are you ready?"

"Yes. Let's do this."

He takes me on stage, and we both pick up a Mic. The music begins, and I turn toward him and wink. Then we start our duet. The song is All I Have by Jennifer Lopez and LL Cool J. The song has nothing to do with our current status, but we still get into it and commit to the performance.

And we nail it. The whole bar is showing us love with whistles and applause as we take our seats.

Karaoke, the only place you can sing off-key, or like a fool and still make people smile. I'm having a blast!

We listen and watch more people fill the bar with their vocals, getting drawn to the melodies and swaying and jamming in our seats. There's slow songs, fast songs, and beats and rhythms in-between those. And by the time Carter and I are ready to get back on the stage, as it's now our turn again, we're feeling the alcohol, tipsy but not drunk.

This should be really good and highly entertaining.

The song is No Diggity by Blackstreet and featuring Dr. Dre and Queen Pen. Carter starts the song with Dr. Dre's opening rap, and some of the patrons get very animated, like it's a real concert. So we go with it. He works the stage, and I stand in the background and dance to the beat.

Then I take center stage and take the first verse, dancing, singing, and filling the stage with my presence, something I know how to do well.

But we both own the chorus, me taking a part and him taking a part. I sing the line "I like the way you work it" and he sings the line "I got to bag it up" and we go back and forth with the line "no diggity" and we turn our attention to each other for the entire chorus.

Then Carter takes center stage and takes the next verse. He fills the stage with his presence, and he's pretty good at it. I'm not the only one that's eyeing him.

The chorus comes around again, and we both own it again, taking our individual parts. And when we sing the line "Hey yo, hey yo, hey yo" everybody in the bar joins us. It's really cool.

Then I take Queen Pen's rap that's toward the end of the song. I try to channel her skills and deliver like she does, and I do alright, not too bad. Carter's manly stare isn't the only one on me.

At the last of the lyrics, more of the chorus and chants, Carter and I are not the only ones singing. The whole entire bar is singing with us, even the bartenders and waitresses. It's beyond cool.

"That was so much fun!" I exclaim, beaming.

"It was," he agrees, smiling just as big as me. "Now let's go and have some sexy fun," he says.

"Dirty, sexy fun," I say, making the correction.

"I'm very intrigued by your mind, Savannah. I can't wait to get you home."

And on that note, Carter pays our bill, gives our waitress a generous tip, and then takes my hand and escorts me out of the bar. And we are in a cab and on the way to my apartment five minutes later.

"You've got me in your domain, Savannah," Carter says, standing in my bedroom, the heat that follows us now filling the air surrounding us. "What are you going to do with me?"

I step up to him, looking in his eyes, and I begin unbuttoning his shirt. His lips part as he stares back into my eyes, and his breathing accelerates a little. I push his shirt off his shoulders, and then I move my fingers to his jeans, my eyes still locked with his. I unbutton and unzip his jeans and yank them down far enough to see his growing erection straining in his boxers. Then I free his cock, grabbing it, and then stroking it up and down. He moans, and I press my lips to his.

I kiss him with dominance, my lechery filling his mouth over and over. I control his tongue with my own, my lust lathering it with lascivious strokes. And our sexual vocals are exchanged back and forth repeatedly.

But he wants to know what I'm going to do with him. Yes, time to mix sexy and dirty together.

His cock is rock solid in my hand, and I break our kiss, pulling my lips off of his. I look into his eyes, both of us with labored breaths. I press a soft kiss on his lips and quickly pull back. "Finish taking your clothes off and get on the bed," I tell him, releasing his cock.

"Damn, Savannah, I see why your sister calls you Little Vixen," he says, taking his shirt off the rest of the way. Yeah, that was sort of mentioned during dinner when we were discussing our families.

I wink at him, and then go to my closet and pull out my box of toys.

"What's in the box?" he asks, taking his socks and shoes off, and then pulling down his boxers and jeans.

"A few dildos, vibrators, and other toys," I reply, opening the box and taking out my lube.

"Why doesn't that surprise me?" he says, grinning.

"Because, like you said, I'm a wild woman," I state.

"You definitely are," he agrees, pulling back my comforter and climbing onto my bed. He sits against my pillows and stares at me, his erection waiting for me.

I set the lube on the bed and gradually begin stripping my clothes off, one piece at a time.

"God, your body is a work of art." His voice is husky, and his cock is twitching.

I slip off my silk bra and panties and climb onto my bed, my eyes locked on his as I do. I sit back on my bended legs, and then I grab his cock, lick my lips, and lower my mouth to the pulsating tip.

"Shit," he voices as I take the head into my mouth. "Fuck," he calls out as I suck on him just a little.

I moan with the head of his cock in my mouth, and then I lower my mouth onto him farther, taking in his hardness and filling my mouth with him. He gasps, and I start to suck him in and out of my warm, wet, tight suction continuously.

He places his hand at my nape, and then slowly moves his hand up and pulls out my ponytail, and my hair falls on my shoulders and down my back. He runs his fingers through my chestnut locks as I suck and suck.

But I'm on a mission to have him fill all my holes, all three, so one down and two more to go. I remove my lips from his cock and climb onto his lap. I stare into his eyes, which are a dark blue now, and I kiss him. I kiss him with a passionate power.

He sits up straight and circles his hands around me and pulls me closer. My breasts are smashed between us, my nipples rubbing against his warm flesh, and I'm beginning to drip in-between my thighs. I want him inside my wetness, filling my pussy.

I break the kiss, but I don't pull back. Instead, I breathe my desire on his lips, and then I lift up slightly, grab his cock, and lower my sex onto him, taking him all the way inside me. I still in his lap as his hard thickness throbs against my inner walls, my walls that are already swelling around him.

Damn, my pussy is in such a craving that I know it won't take much for me to come.

Carter squeezes my backside and holds onto my ass cheeks as I begin to move up and down. He moans, and I moan, and we continue moaning on each other's lips as I rise and fall on his cock.

I move my hands around his neck and revel in the way he feels and fits inside me, and in the way his hands hold me to him. It's like he was made for me, crafted perfectly to suit my body in every way.

"Savannah, oh, Savannah," he moans and moans on my lips while squeezing my cheeks over and over in his strong hands.

God, I love hearing him say my name, especially in the middle of ecstasy. It makes me wetter, and it makes my inner walls cling to him.

"You're so tight," he says, his voice rough. "God, Savannah, I'm about to come."

"Oh yes," I breathe. I'm right there with him as I continue to swallow his cock with my up and down movements.

He digs his fingers into my ass. He moans really loud, and then I feel him throb really hard inside me, releasing his nut.

I fall down hard on his cock and release my own cream all over him and in his lap. "Oh, Carter," I breathe, and then I kiss him.

I kiss him and kiss him, and he's still hard inside me. He squeezes my entire body, crushing me to him, and a big quiver ripples throughout my frame and has me vibrating in his arms.

"Two down and just one more to go," my inner vixen whispers.

He's occupied my mouth. He's occupied my pussy. Now I want him to occupy my ass.

"Carter," I murmur on his lips. "Carter, I want you inside my ass." I start lifting up and releasing him from my warm wetness.

He instantly releases his grip on me, and I climb off him. There's something I want to do first, and then I'll climb back on him and take us for a wild ride.

I scoot down his body and begin licking his cock, licking all my juices off him, from the base to the tip and all around. And although he's still hard, he gets harder, rock hard again.

"Oh fuck," he blurts out. "You're amazing."

"I'm not done with you yet." I climb up his body and settle into his lap again.

"Dirty, sexy fun," he says, gazing into my eyes.

I nod. "Filling each of my holes," I say.

"Hot damn, you wild woman," he says, and smacks my ass.

I grab the lube, squirt a nice amount into my palm, and then I coat Carter's cock with it. "Ready?" I ask, rubbing the rest of the lube from my palm all around my anus.

"Hell yeah," he says, grinning.

I place one hand on his shoulder, and I grab his cock with my other hand. I lift up, position him at my hole, and then very slowly lower myself onto him.

I bite my bottom lip and stare into his eyes as I gradually and carefully sink into his lap. His lips part, his eyes glaze over in a smoldering heat, and he grabs my backside with both hands again. Then I start to slowly move up and down, taking all of his length in my ass over and over.

"God, Savannah," he murmurs. "Shit."

I move my hands around his neck, gripping him. Then I kiss him with the same hot authority that my lips have been giving him all night. And he grips and squeezes my backside the same way he's been doing all night. And our hot intensity makes this hot act of anal sex extremely impassioned.

We're both moaning into each other's mouths, and we're both fairly loud. Our grips on one another are fierce, getting stronger and stronger in haste. My clit is swollen and hard from the fire between us, and I'm on the verge of climaxing with every one of his moans that enters my mouth. His cock is very swollen and very hard from my tight anal grasp, and I know my moans into his mouth are affecting him, too.

My mouth is fucking him. My ass is fucking him. I'm fucking him oh so dirty, sexy, good.

The vehemence consumes us entirely, and we climax together, moaning thunderous pleasures all over our fervent lips.

My inner vixen lays spent across her sheets with a smile on her face as her eyes roll to the back of her head.

Carter is the explosive fireworks and hot, untamed passion that I've longed for in my life. I just hope we can continue to make this work, because we're in for a wild romance.

Chapter Eleven

"This is a sweet setup, Carter." I'm in his home and admiring it. He lives in a loft with a great view of Lake Michigan.

It's the day after our dirty, sexy fun, and we've both been smiling nonstop. We went to bed smiling. We woke up smiling. We smiled all through breakfast. And we're still smiling into the afternoon.

"Yeah, I got a good deal on it, too," he says, setting up our lunch at his kitchen island. We're having takeout, subs from Potbelly Sandwich Shop. Carter got the Italian, and I got the Turkey Breast.

I'm looking out his windows and watching the boats in the distance that are on the lake. It really is a cool view.

Carter gave me a quick tour as soon as we got here. It's a very spacious place, yet not overly huge. There's a living area, a separate area where he creates his art, a kitchen, and an entire wall that is made of three really big windows overlooking the water. His bedroom is up a staircase, a loft inside his loft. It's very cool and open, the whole place is.

"Let's eat," he announces.

I join him and sit next to him on a stool, me on the corner side of the island and him next to me, but diagonally next me as he's on the other side of the corner. We can look directly at each other this way, and we begin eating our lunch, which is very tasty. And in my opinion, these are the best subs in all of Chicago. They're delish.

"What's your favorite color?" he asks me, setting down his beer, a Beck's beer.

"Red." I smile. "I love red."

He smiles back at me. "That's my favorite color, too."

"Really," I voice, sounding just a little surprised. "Do you favor that color in your paintings?" I ask him.

Carter has just two of his paintings displayed on the walls in his home. One is of a tiger in the jungle. The tiger is big and ferocious with its orange, black, and bits of white colors deep and notable, its teeth powerful and dangerous, and there's a sun in the painting that is bright red. The other painting is of a flight of birds that are soaring over the ocean. The birds are all black with large wings, and the ocean is a midnight blue with a small, gray moon in the distance. They're extremely beautiful and all impressive.

"Not particularly," he says, "although, I do have a painting at my gallery that I painted using only reds, a few different shades of red."

"Well, red suits you, Carter. It's the color of strength, power, and determination."

"It's also the color of passion, desire, and love. It's perfect for you, Savannah, plus it looks great on you."

"You're trying to make my cheeks turn red," I tease.

"I like it when your plump, round cheeks turn red from my touch," he says, his eyes serious and staring into mine.

"I like that, too." I bite my bottom lip. Hmm, maybe he'll smack my ass some more tonight, or sooner than tonight.

He doesn't say anything, but he continues to stare at me while taking a bite of his sub, and then taking a drink of his beer. It's intense, and I want to know what he's thinking, but then he finally speaks. "I want to show you the rest of my paintings."

"You're taking me to your gallery?" I stare at him a little wider, sounding more surprised now.

"Yes, right after we finish our lunch."

"Oh cool, I'm excited." I smile and grab my beer.

Just then, Carter's cell phone rings. "Excuse me, Savannah," he says, picking up his phone. "Hey, man," he speaks into his phone.

I patiently wait and eat my food while he talks, and he doesn't keep me waiting long. It's a quick conversation.

"We'll be by in an hour or so," he says into his phone. "Take it easy," he says, and ends the call.

"We're going somewhere else?" I ask.

"We are," he replies. "That was my brother. He and his wife are sick. They've both got strep throat and feel like hell, but they have tickets to a concert tonight, so they are giving us the tickets."

"The only concert in town that I know about is Fall Out Boy."

"That's the one."

"Oh sweet, I've never seen them in concert."

"So, you're a fan then?" he inquires.

"I am." I smile.

"Good, so am I."

"We're going to have so much fun!" I bounce a little on my stool.

We finish up our lunch in an effortless conversation, learning more of one another's interests and of our shared likes. It turns out that we have even more similarities in our worlds. Not only do we have common ground in the arts and in the beauty of the arts, but also in music, food, and physical outdoor activities. It's refreshing and compelling at the same time. We're both free spirits.

*   *   *   *   *   *   *   *

"Wow, Carter, this is even greater than I imagined," I say as we enter his gallery.

Carter's name is on the outside of the building, which is located on the corner of a busy street in downtown Chicago and looking remarkable. His name is stenciled in big, black, cursive letters, and two of the walls are gigantic windows. And like his home, this setup is sweet as well.

"Hey, Carter," a hip looking guy says, as Carter and I are fully in his element now.

"Hey, Dylan," Carter greets him. "This is Savannah Lewis," he tells him, and then he turns his head to me and says, "This is my assistant, Dylan Jacobs."

Dylan steps to me and offers me his hand. "Hi, Savannah, it's nice to meet you."

"Hi, it's nice to meet you, too," I say, shaking his hand.

"Wait a minute," Dylan says, releasing my hand. "You're the poetess from Intoxication."

"I am." I smile at him.

"My boyfriend told me about you. He's bringing me to Intoxication next Friday to hear your "naughty scribblings" as he calls it."

I giggle. I like that reference to what I do. "Cool."

"How's business today, Dylan? Anybody come in here yet today?" Carter asks him.

Dylan's whole face lights up. "A painting sold today, the one of Paris at night in the winter."

"Excellent," Carter says. Then he turns to me and says, "Go ahead and take a look around. I just need to handle some paperwork." He kisses my cheek. "I won't be long."

"Okay," I say, and he walks into his back room.

I begin to gradually walk around the gallery and appreciate all of the art. There are paintings covering the walls all around, plus there are some drawings and sketches mixed in as well. And I'm in complete awe as my eyes take in every color, every shape, and the meaning of Carter's work. He's brilliant, and his work is beautiful, actually priceless if you ask me.

He has many pieces of artwork that are of his perspective of cities from all over the world. Plus, there's so much more. There's artwork of different kinds and types of wildlife. There's artwork of all kinds of magnificent nature. There's artwork of people in different sceneries and scenarios, some energetic, some casual, some emotional, some of loving embraces, some of sexy embraces, and some that are very, very erotic. And there is one erotic painting that I'm completely captivated by.

"It's incredible, isn't it?" Dylan says, speaking of the painting that has my total attention.

I'm mesmerized by Carter's all red painting, all red and as erotic as my words. It is a few different shades of red, just as Carter said it was. And it's almost like one of the scenes from one of my books jumped out and landed on his canvas. It's amazing, not only beautiful but sexy and hot. I love it.

"It's stunning," I voice. It's a depiction of a man and a woman in the throes of passion and ecstasy.

"It's new," Dylan informs me. "In fact, most of his sexual forms of artwork are from the last two months," he adds.

Hmm, that's very interesting. Two months ago is exactly when me and Carter's paths crossed and combined. He's been a constant in my thoughts and dreams since then, and it seems as though he's been overwhelmed by our connection, too.

"That's what he told me anyways when I asked him about these particular pieces," Dylan says. Then he leans in a little closer and says, "I'm guessing you're his muse."

I turn my head slightly and look at him. "Maybe," I say, and then I give him a smile and a wink.

"Uh-huh, I thought so as soon as you walked in here with him."

Before I can respond, Carter is back. "All my loose ends are taken care of," he says. "Are you ready, Savannah?"

"Yeah," I nod.

He grabs my hand, threading his fingers through mine. "I'll see you soon, Dylan."

"Bye, Carter, bye, Savannah," Dylan says, grinning.

"Bye," I say, and wave as Carter and I exit his gallery.

Carter hails us a cab. He gives the driver the address to where we are going, and then we are on our way.

"Your paintings, your drawings, your sketches, they are all amazing," I tell Carter, smiling brightly.

"Thank you," he replies with a nice smile of his own.

"Your artwork tells me that you've been to many places, seen a lot of things, and had some wonderful experiences."

"I have," he agrees.

"Like all those different cities."

"About three years ago, I went to Europe and traveled through many cities of a few countries, plus I traveled a lot of Europe's countryside on a motorcycle. I left with a single backpack that only contained clothes, toiletries, and money, and I came back with a photographic memory of everything I saw, experienced, and witnessed."

"That is awesome, so cool."

"Yeah, I met some fascinating people along the way also."

"Do you keep in touch with any of them?"

"No," he says. "I just had small talk throughout my travels. I was basically just trying to escape realty."

"All part of your ability of being good at being alone," I state, recalling what he said to me in Hawaii.

"Exactly," he says. "You remember everything I've told you, don't you?"

"I do." I smile, and his mouth curls into a smile, too. Then he kisses my cheek, but I grab his chin as his lips linger, and I pull his mouth to mine. I give him a hard but infatuating kiss.

"I want you in my bed tonight," he says, his voice really deep.

"I would love to leave my scent on your sheets and the memory of me outlined in them also." Just like he's done to my bed, I want his bed to have the lasting effects of our sexy relations, too.

"Damn, Savannah, I love the way you talk."

There's not really anything to say to that. It's just the way I am. It's just who I am. So I change the subject. "I love your red painting."

"It's actually one of my favorites."

"I see why. It's very red, very sexy, and very hot."

"Thank you," he says with a grin.

"Dylan assumes I'm your muse."

"Dylan's right," he admits. "I left you in Hawaii, but you didn't leave me."

Whoa! That is enlightening. And a little more of his mystery is gone with a simple statement.

That disclosure lingers around us as the cab stops at our destination.

Carter asks the cab driver to wait since we'll only be a minute, and then takes my hand in his, helping me out of the cab, and then threading his fingers through mine. Then he leads me up a few stairs to the cluster homes that we've arrived at. He knocks on the door, and we wait.

"Hey, man," his brother, who looks a lot like him but a bit older, says as he opens his front door.

"Hey, Caleb," Carter says. "This is Savannah Lewis." Then he turns his head toward me and says, "Savannah, this is my brother, Caleb."

"Hi, Savannah," Caleb says. "It's nice to finally meet you. I would love to give you a hug, but I don't want any of my germs to come in contact with you."

"It's that bad?" Carter questions him, lifting an eyebrow. Then he pulls me inside the foyer as Caleb moves aside for us to enter.

"Yeah," Caleb replies. "Ashley and I just started our antibiotics for the strep throat yesterday, but she also has pink eye, and it's nasty, man. She's in pretty bad shape. She's asleep right now."

"That sucks. I'm sorry about your luck, man," Carter says.

"Yeah, I'm sorry, too, but I'm glad to meet you," I say with a small smile.

"We'll live. Ashley wanted to meet you, too, but she'd rather meet you when she doesn't look and feel like hell," Caleb tells me. "Maybe we can all have dinner once Ashley and I are back to normal," he adds.

"I'd like that," I say.

"Yeah, that sounds good," Carter agrees.

"Well, here are the tickets," Caleb says, reaching into his pocket and pulling them out. He hands them to Carter.

"Thanks," Carter says, slipping them into his pocket.

"Thank you, Caleb." I smile. "Please tell Ashley thank you as well."

"I sure will. You guys have fun, and I want to hear all about it."

"I'll bring you two back some souvenirs," Carter assures him.

"Great," Caleb says. "I'm going to get back to bed now."

We say our goodbyes, and then Carter escorts me back into the cab. The cab driver pulls into traffic, and Carter pulls me close, placing his arm around my shoulders. The heat between us rises, and a couple flames ignite. Then Carter cracks the window, allowing a tiny breeze to mix with our small-scale fire.

"You seem to make everywhere we go twenty degrees hotter, especially when we're in an enclosed space."

"No, we seem to," I correct him. "It's what happens whenever we're in the same room. We don't even have to be touching. It's just us."

"You're right. It's been present ever since I met you in Hawaii."

"And it's been following us ever since." I take a somewhat deep breath and blow it out, preparing myself for the little extra that I'm about to add. "You've been starring in my dreams ever since we met, too."

"Oh, Savannah, I've been dreaming about you, too." He takes my chin into his free hand, turning my face to his, and he kisses me. "My paintings," he murmurs against my mouth.

"My writings," I breathe on his lips, and then our kiss deepens.

Our kiss ignites more flames, and the cab driver cracks all the windows down two or three inches.

*   *   *   *   *   *   *   *

"Ooh, let's do it," I urge him, squeezing his hand.

Carter and I have had a couple of exciting hours since our intense and overly warm cab drive. We didn't go back to his place or mine. We wanted to have some fun, and by the look in his eyes, I automatically knew there would be some risqué fun involved. And I love our spontaneity together, plus I like to take a risk sometimes. So we went to the Skydeck, braved the glass balcony, took pictures with our phones, and had a great time. We had a sexy and naughty moment in that time as well.

When we first arrived there, we were beyond horny, and there was a wait for the glass balcony. So Carter pulled me into a janitor's office, locked the door, pulled down my jeans, pulled my thong to the side, and fucked me from the back. He moaned in my ear the entire time, and I moaned, too. It's was so hot, and we both came so hard.

"Really, are you sure?" he asks me.

After the Skydeck, we shared a big banana split that included chocolate ice cream, vanilla ice cream, strawberry ice cream, lots of whip cream, four slices of bananas, and cherries on top. We had a couple of shots, but mostly we washed it down with beer after beer. And now I'm feeling the alcohol.

"Yes, come on," I urge him more, squeezing his hand again and tugging on him slightly.

We've been walking around, and we're stopped in front of a tattoo parlor. We still have plenty of time before the concert starts, and this is something I've wanted to do. Neither one of us has any tattoos, so why not.

"Alright," he says, grinning, "after you, Miss Lewis."

Carter opens the door for me, and I enter with him right behind me. We're immediately greeted and taken into a separate room. I know exactly what I want, so I go first.

I brace myself for the pain, and Carter takes my hand in his, threading his fingers through mine. "You can squeeze as hard as you need to," he tells me.

I nod at him, and then I close my eyes.

"Shit!" I loudly blurt out. It feels like a thousand tiny needles are stabbing me over and over. Even with the alcohol in me, it still hurts. But I squeeze Carter's hand and suck it up. I can do this.

And after about forty five minutes, my tattoos are complete. I got two, one behind my ear, and the other along the arch of my foot.

"They look great, Savannah," Carter says, smiling. "And sexy, too," he adds.

I got three tiny, red hearts behind my right ear, and I got a romantic quote in all black cursive letters along the outside of my left foot. It reads: The soul, the kiss, the heart; the first words of love.

I'm happy with my tattoos and how they turned out, and I can't wait for them to heal, so I can show them off.

Now it's Carter's turn. He came up with something different as well, and it's perfect for him. I take his hand as his tattoo begins. He doesn't make any noise, and he keeps his eyes open, his head turned toward me, and his eyes locked on mine. I barely blink. It's a great and special moment.

The entire event, my tattoos and his, results in a significant bonding experience between us. It's evident in our eyes. It's written all over our faces. We've grown closer, and we both know it.

"It's so cool," I voice.

Carter got a tattoo on the inside of his left bicep. It's a rough looking feather. The feathers are blowing away, one by one, but they're turning into a flight of birds as they scatter. The whole tattoo is black ink, but the birds have red-tipped wings, and there's a three word quote below the image. It reads: creativity takes courage.

He's smiling, showing his teeth. He's happy with the way his tattoo turned out also.

Carter pays for our tattoos, even though I told him I'd pay for my own, but he insisted until I agreed. So I left a very generous tip for the tattoo artist, who was really appreciative.

Carter hails us a cab. A Fall Out Boy song comes on the radio, Irresistible. We ask the driver to turn it up, and we get hyped for our next stop, seeing them live!

* * * * * * * *

"Excuse me," Carter begins, "can I borrow your lighter?" he asks a young guy that's smoking with a group of people.

We're in the parking lot of the venue, and I just scored two joints from a chic that was giving them away for free. She was a total hippie and so damn nice. And that's usually the norm with hippies, kind, charitable, giving, and just plain happy people.

The weed smells really good, too. Hippies usually have the best recreational drugs. And we're about to find out.

Carter lights my joint, then his. "Thanks," he tells the guy, handing him back the lighter.

"No problem," the guy replies.

Carter takes my hand, threading his fingers through, and we walk to a nearby tree and sit down against it. We puff on our joints and watch the people partying all over the parking lot. The weed is smooth and clean. It's very good.

"Do you smoke often, Savannah?" Carter asks me.

"Not too often," I state. "Lacy will bring some home every once in a while and share it with me. How about you, do you smoke regularly?"

"Not really," he says, "just every once in a while, like you."

"Do you get inspired at all when you smoke?"

"I do sometimes." He smiles. "When my state of mind is good, I usually get really creative from it."

"Same here," I agree. "It fills my mind with so many words and so many potential stories."

"Damn, Savannah, everything I learn about you..." He grins and shakes his head a bit. "You're like the other half of me."

I smile at him. "And do you feel whole now?"

"Every time I'm with you..." He nods. "Yes."

We're both smiling, from ear to ear, at each other.

We finish our joints, and then head into the concert as the opening act, a new and upcoming band, is performing their last song.

Carter gets us each a tall glass of beer, and then we find our seats, which aren't too bad. We're eighteen rows back from the stage and off to the mid-right of the stage. I can see everything rather clearly from my seat, and even more clearly if I stand, which I'm sure I will be doing all night.

Fall Out Boy music begins behind the curtain, the drums and guitars. Then the curtain is literally ripped down, and the band appears, full of energy, starting the show immediately. They start with their song Uma Thurman, and absolutely everyone is out of their seats, Carter and I included, rocking out to the beat.

"I love this song!" I shout.

"Me, too, it's a great song!" Carter shouts.

Fall Out Boy is fucking awesome! We're having a blast. The band keeps the hits coming. Carter keeps the beers coming. And I keep dancing all around and all over Carter. He's moving to the rhythms, too, dancing with me.

The band plays so many of their songs. They perform My Songs Know What You Did in the Dark, The Phoenix, Sugar, We're Goin Down, Dance, Dance, Church, Centuries, I Don't Care, Alone Together, Nobody Puts Baby in the Corner, A Little Less Sixteen Candles, a Little More "Touch Me", Irresistible, plus so many more. I think they cover every song of theirs that's ever been played on the radio, plus ones that haven't. And they sound sensational, their voices and their instruments.

By the end of the show, Carter and I are drunk, our weed buzzes are fading, our ears are ringing, but big smiles are plastered on our faces.

We pick up souvenirs as we leave. Carter buys four t-shirts, one for me, one for himself, one for his brother, and one for his sister-in-law. He also gets Ashley a signed picture of the band, and he gets Caleb a signed CD that he doesn't already own. I purchase two extra t-shirts, different from the others, one for me and one for Carter. Then we exit the venue.

Before we get into a cab, we stop by a food truck. It's a macaroni and cheese food truck. We each get the same thing, The Mac topped with applewood smoked bacon, fresh tomatoes, and green onions. We also get bottles of water. The food soaks up some of the alcohol, satisfies our munchies, and it's quite tasty.

The cab ride back to Carter's loft is all touching and feeling as our hands are all over each other, our lips, too, stealing kiss after kiss. And by the time the driver pulls up to Carter's place, I have his belt undone, along with the button and zipper on his jeans. And he has the button on my jeans undone, the zipper unzipped just a tad, plus his hands are up my shirt and unhooking my bra. We arrive just in time, before clothes begin to be swiftly removed.

We stagger through the door, and we scurry with one another's clothing, throwing it all over. And this is how the rest of our evening goes, locked tightly in passion, driven by desire, and consumed by lust.

"Oh, Savannah," he moans.

"Carter, oh, Carter," I moan and moan.

And not only do I leave my scent embedded into his sheets, I leave my climaxes staining them in a few spots. The memory of me is all over his room.

Chapter Twelve

"Yuck," I voice as I'm looking out Carter's huge windows. "It's nasty and ugly outside."

It's Monday morning. We've just concluded our breakfast, in which we both found ourselves humming the upbeat tunes from last night's concert in-between our bites of food, plus last night's hot and sexy preoccupation with each other was still floating in the air. That made for a nice breakfast, especially since our view isn't very nice today. It's raining hard, and the winds are dangerously strong. And I don't want to step out in that.

"Stay with me all day," Carter says, stepping behind me and circling me in his arms. He kisses my neck, then my shoulder, and then my neck again.

The heat begins to spread through my body, and my inner vixen yawns and pulls her silk sheet off her body, exposing her naked flesh and opening her legs.

"Don't you have to work today?"

"My gallery is closed on Mondays and Tuesdays, and I currently feel like painting your body with my tongue."

I turn in his arms and place my arms around his neck. "I'd love to be your canvas." I kiss his lips softly.

"You don't have to help out at your parents' store, do you?"

"No. I usually help out on Tuesdays, Wednesdays, and sometimes on Thursdays. And as long as you have a notebook and a pen, then I'm all set."

"I do." His lips curl into a sexy grin.

"Then I'm all yours." I kiss him again.

"I like the sound of that," he murmurs on my lips, then deepens the kiss and hugs me tighter. And after a hot minute, he pulls back and stares into my eyes. "I know the view isn't anything nice to look at, but I want to make love to you right here. I don't want to move."

"I'm good with that. I actually love the rain."

"Really," he says, cocking his head, his eyes widening.

"Yes." I smile. "I know I said it's ugly out, and it is, but I've always found the sounds of raindrops to be soothing and the sounds of a thunderstorm to be exciting."

"Do you like to play in the rain, too?"

"I do, but with these tornado-like winds and the new tattoos, it's not a good idea today."

"True," he agrees.

I turn my head to the side, looking out the window again. "If you look out far enough though, you can see the beauty of the storm, the rain hitting the water, the high winds making the waves crash into each other, and the sky as it turns darker, making the water look almost black."

"Spoken like a true artist," he says.

I turn my head back to him, looking in his eyes. "It's a yucky, nasty day because we can't have any fun outside."

"But that makes for a fun time inside." He smirks at me in a playful and sexy way.

"It does." I bite my bottom lip.

He brings his thumb to my lip, gently pulling it free, and then he kisses me. "With your beauty," he murmurs on my lips.

"And our heat," I whisper into our kiss.

"Fun all over my loft," he murmurs on my lips, and then he deepens our kiss, sliding his tongue in and tasting mine.

We kiss fervidly, me tight in his arms, and he begins backing me into the window wall, considerately pressing me into it. Then he lifts up his white t-shirt that I'm wearing. He lifts it up to my waist, exposing my naked pussy and backside. He slides his hand into his boxer briefs, pulling them down a little and releasing his hard cock. Then he breaks our kiss, pressing his forehead against mine, both of us panting.

I hook my leg around him. "Fuck me hard first, and then make love to me." My voice is breathy and a bit strangled sounding as I pant.

"Shit," he breathes. "You've read my mind." He grabs his cock and pushes it inside me, and we both gasp as he fills me.

"Oh god, I love the change of plans." He's crushed against my body, glued to me in my clutching grip. And I'm crushed against the glass, taking in every hard, pounding inch of him as the rain smacks the window with solid, unyielding raindrops. "Hard first," I breathe.

"Then soft," he says, rubbing my thigh that's securely fastened around him.

A loud moan escapes my mouth. My inner walls flutter around him. And I'm soaking wet, coating his cock, dripping into his groin.

He moves his hand to my backside. "I like my shirt on you. It's incredibly sexy." He kisses me hard. "But take it off. I want to see you. I want to feel your tits smashed against me."

Oh fuck. My inner walls flutter around him again.

Carter stills inside me, and I quickly pull his t-shirt over my head, dropping it on the floor. Then I move my hands back around his neck, grasping him, smashing my breasts between our warm flesh, and he begins to fill me hard all over again, the same forceful grinds.

We're both panting and gazing at each other. We're both completely and utterly open to one another, our emotions surrounding us, right along with a blazing fire. We are undoubtedly obsessed with each other's passion and full of deep affection. It's evident all around us and reflecting from our eyes. We're falling for one another, and falling fast.

And I don't want anyone else but him.

"Am I the only naked woman that's been here in your loft?" I have to know. He's been the only man in my bed since I met him.

"Yes, and I intend to keep it that way." He thrusts in me hard, so hard, gripping my backside and placing his other hand on the glass behind me, his palm flat against it.

"Oh, Carter," I breathe, my entire pussy fluttering, inside and out, my walls, my lips, absolutely all of it.

"Savannah," he whispers. "My Savannah," he whispers again, then kisses me uncontrollably.

My whole entire body starts to shake against him and against the window, and then I come. I come hard and all around him. I moan and moan and moan into his mouth as big ripples of ecstasy run through me.

Carter breaks the kiss and watches me come for him, continuing to pound my sex. "Savannah." He digs his fingers into my backside. "I love how your pussy takes my dick and doesn't want to let it go."

I'm panting too much to speak, riding out the end of my orgasm.

"Come for me again. She wants it." He stares into my eyes and thrusts in and out, in and out. "I want it."

"Oh, Carter, oh, Carter," I manage to form words in gasping breaths in-between my heavy panting, my entire pussy still fluttering all around him.

"My Savannah," he murmurs, then kisses me with wild desire, causing his thrusts to be more powerful with every hard stroke inside my wet, very wet warmth.

And just as my orgasm concludes, another one begins, and I shake in ecstasy once more, clinging to Carter.

He swallows my moans, loud and continuous moans. He pounds into me, moans all over our untamed lips, and then he comes inside me. He removes his hand from the glass, grabbing my other ass cheek with it and digging his fingers into my skin. And he keeps kissing me with an unrestrained tongue as we climax together.

And then it's time for slow, making love with one another.

"I want to make you come again," he says, lightly caressing my cheek with his knuckles.

"I've never been with a man that can make me come without me helping my orgasm along," I admit, my voice a little breathy.

"Really," he says, his voice husky, slowing withdrawing his cock as I remove my leg from around him.

"Really," I nod.

"Sex with you blows my mind, Savannah. I'm altogether addicted. I want all of your orgasms."

Whoa. That is hot, and it makes me wetter.

"I want to give them all to you, Carter," I declare. Then his lips are on mine, kissing me heatedly.

Suddenly, the power goes out, and we slow down the kiss, and then pull our lips apart.

"I'll go light some candles, get some blankets, and get some pillows," he says. The storm has it looking like night. It's dark.

"Ooh, romantic," I state, smiling.

"Very," he agrees, and then gives me a quick kiss. "Don't move," he adds, and smiles.

Carter takes his boxers off the rest of the way, and then moves around his loft, lighting small candles and gathering a few blankets and pillows from an antique wood chest. He begins laying the blankets out in front of the big window wall, and then places the pillows on top. Then he's back at my lips again.

He kisses me softly and scoops me up into his arms. "Let's go, Gorgeous," he says, then drops another kiss on my lips.

I bring my hands to his cheeks and brush over them with my fingers and deepen the kiss a little with soft, sensual movements of my lips and a little teasing with my tongue. We both quietly moan, and then I pull back. He lowers me onto the blankets, releases me, and just gazes into my eyes.

"I love your taste," he says. "Your lips," he says, slowly brushing his thumb over my top lip, and then my bottom lip, as my mouth is slightly open. "These lips, too," he says, slowing gliding his fingers down my body, stopping at my sex, and sliding two inside me, swirling them around, and then moving them in and out.

I moan and moan as I gaze back at him.

"So good," he says, and kisses my mouth, tasting my moans and my tongue. Then he withdraws his fingers, releases my whimpering mouth, brings his fingers to his mouth, and sucks my taste off of each one.

I drip onto the blankets as I watch him.

"I love your taste," he repeats, his eyes darkening to a deep blue sea. And I'm lost at sea. "My Savannah," he adds.

"Oh god, Carter, make love to me," I beg, my breathing just a bit strained.

He kisses my lips. "I think we need a few more candles. I want to see every single ravishing inch of your body." He rises and walks to his kitchen.

I'm so turned on, I begin touching and feeling myself.

I move my hands over my breasts, squeezing them, and then my nipples. Then I move one hand down to my wet warmth and push two fingers inside, pushing them in and out. Fondling my body, penetrating my body, I can't keep quiet about it, so I give Carter an earful before he gets an eyeful.

"Touching myself... I wait... Dripping for you... I wait... Desire pulsing through my veins... Hot pools of lust coating my fingers... I wait..."

Carter rapidly appears in front of me, almost dropping the candles in his hands.

"I'm waiting," I breathe, giving him an eyeful.

"Fuck," he says, his eyes taking me all in. Then he quickly turns and sets the candles on top of small towels at the window wall. He lights them, sets the lighter down, and is between my legs within seconds.

I withdraw my fingers and stick them in my mouth. And before I know it, Carter is lowering his head and licking between my folds, my very wet folds. I moan on my fingers.

My moaning becomes louder and louder as I watch him, and then I sink into the pillows and blankets.

His tongue licks through my slit. His tongue dips inside my pussy. His skilled tongue paints his love for it over and over.

"Oh, Carter, oh Carter," I moan and moan.

He looks up at me, capturing my eyes, and continues to paint my sex with his tongue. Then my legs start shaking, and I come, and he licks it all into his mouth.

"Addiction," he murmurs, oh so slowly licking up my body, painting his love for it on my belly, my breasts, my nipples, and my neck. "Being devoted to my passion for you," he murmurs, staring down into my eyes, the head of his cock already entering me.

"Addicted," I whisper.

"Completely," he whispers back, and then pushes the rest of his cock inside me. We both moan, and I wrap my body around him as he begins to thrust in me deeply, but nice, slow, and softly.

"You're so deep, and it feels so good," I murmur, my breathing turning into panting.

"Deeper," he says, his voice husky, and he grabs my thigh and pushes my bent leg into me, and his cock fills me even deeper.

"Oh!" I call out, and my whole body quivers. "Oh!"

"So deep inside a gorgeous beauty," he murmurs. "My sexy poetess," he adds, and my body quivers again.

He fucks so good. He feels so good. He fills me deeper than I've ever been filled before.

My body quivers yet again, but this time doesn't stop, and I come all around his hardness and all over the blankets underneath me, moaning, panting, and gripping his shoulders.

"It takes my breath away watching you come," he says, his voice huskier as he thrusts so deep.

"Come... Carter... Fill...your...addiction..." I say in-between my panting.

"Fuck," he breathes, thrusting deep, and then he comes very, very deep inside me. He kisses my neck, sucking on it, too. Then he whispers in my ear, "So good."

And we don't move, and we barely blink as we come down from ecstasy.

Then Carter releases his grip on my thigh, but we stay enfolded in each other's arms, staring into one another's eyes, and basking in our heat.

"I don't want this to end," I admit, my breathing beginning to even out.

"It doesn't have to," he says, and then he kisses me, long, deep, and vehemently.

He throbs against my inner walls, and I know he'll take me deep and fill his addiction for the rest of the day.

And that's exactly what I want.

Chapter Thirteen

"Your words may possess me tonight," Carter warns me, grinning very seductively at me.

"Ooh, I really like the sound of that."

"There's no telling what I may do to you," he adds.

"I can't wait." I wink at him.

He opens the door to Intoxication, and we walk in, him directly behind me. Then he grabs my waist and stops us in our tracks. He says, right at my ear, "Plus, your choice of clothing makes me want to rip every piece off of you."

"Damn, I like the sound of that, too." Jesus, he's awakening my core, my inner vixen, and the flood gates of my cream. I'll just have to let it fuel my performance.

It's Friday night, and it's been four weeks since Carter emerged from the crowd in this very bar, and we've gotten to know one another immensely, on every level. We've stimulated each other's minds. We've captured each other's hearts. And our bodies have made a lot of beautiful and breathtaking art together. It's been a total whirlwind romance, and our flames are burning even hotter and stronger now. We've claimed one another.

In these past weeks, we've become a part of each other's families, too. We've had dinner with Lacy and Brian. We've had dinner with Abby and Steve. We've had dinner with Caleb and Ashley. And we've had dinner with my parents. I even got to meet his parents through Face Time. We also hung out with our siblings and their significant others as a group a few times. Plus, my parents had a barbecue one Saturday afternoon and invited everyone, my small immediate family and his, which was great fun and great bonding between us all. My family loves him, and his family loves me, too. It's nice, definitely ideal.

And our dates together, just the two of us, have been so much fun. We've laughed and played with each other, enjoying the sunshine as we engaged in the outdoors. We rented bicycles and rode along the Lakefront Trail of Lake Michigan. We went kayaking on the lake. We took a helicopter ride that flew us over Lake Michigan and all around Chicago. We went zip lining right outside of the city. We went hiking outside of the city, too, and we had a picnic, plus we gave nature a sexy show. And he took me on a horse and carriage ride through the city one warm evening, in which there was a romantic dinner to follow, plus a night of passion. I have had the best and most thrilling dates with Carter, and the thrills just keep coming.

I took him to my parents' store, too, just to show him, but we did pick up a few items while we were there. I own a ton of toys. I love them. So we picked up a lot of edible underwear, panties and bras, and Carter loves devouring them off my body. My parents' store has them for men, too, so I've been enjoying eating them off of him as well. And of course, I've showed him my box of toys, and we've played with some of them. But we don't really need them. We're more than enough for each other. Our heat is proof of that.

"You are the sexiest woman in the entire universe," he says, still right at my ear.

I'm wearing minimal clothing and feeling explicitly X-rated. I'm dressed in very, very short red Guess shorts, a black satin bra with an extremely thin and extremely black see-through top on, and red bottom heels. My cleavage is fully on display, and my ass cheeks are kind of threatening to peek out, especially if I bend over. I'm ready to drive my audience wild.

And Carter's already there, driving into the wild and stepping on the gas at full speed.

I turn around, his hands still on my waist. "Easy stud, we have to get through tonight first." I give him a chaste kiss. But he gives me another one, and then he gives me a juicy one on the neck. Then he growls on my neck and gives me another juicy kiss there while he squeezes my hips.

"Maybe not," he says, looking into my eyes.

"What do you mean?"

"I may just sneak you into one of the management offices and bend you over a desk in-between your performances."

"Really," I say, my eyes growing wide, and my inner vixen is slipping on a short skirt and nodding enthusiastically.

"I might. You're too tempting." He lowers a hand and squeezes my backside, and then trails his finger from his other hand in-between my breasts. "So fucking tempting," he murmurs, staring into my eyes.

"The aficionado of Savannah," I state. "You'll have to find a way to steal me away from my fans."

"I like a challenge," he says, his sapphires darkening.

I give him a quick kiss. "Come on, Mr. Bennett, let's take some shots."

Carter gives me another kiss, and then takes my hand in his, threading his fingers through. We begin walking toward the bar, but stop at a table first and say hello to Lacy and Brian and Caleb and Ashley. They've all become close, especially Lacy and Brian. He's tamed her and engulfed her with a commitment, and she is really happy. And I'm happy for them.

"I'm excited, Little Vixen, you look ready to slay," Lacy says, smiling at me.

"She does," Ashley agrees. "You look like a hot dose of sexual persuasion," she tells me.

Carter squeezes my hand firmly at that comment.

"I'm mixing a whole lot of sin with my sexy tonight." I wink at Lacy, and then smirk mischievously at everyone. And Lacy returns a wink with a knowing smile.

After chatting with the four of them for a few minutes, we continue to the bar. I sit down next to Abby, who is watching her man at work, and Carter sits down next to me. And like my sister and her man and Carter's brother and his wife, Carter and I have become super close to Abby and Steve. Don't get me wrong, all eight of us are very close, but with Abby being my best friend, it was only natural that Carter gravitated to my sister from another mother and her man. And Abby and I are so giggly-happy about it. We've always dreamed that one day our boyfriends would be close.

Steve sets down two shots of whiskey in front of me and two shots of whiskey in front of Carter. We both swallow down one shot, and then we conversate with the two lovebirds, but quickly break into two different conversations. Carter and Steve fall into their own discussion, and Abby and I turn to each other and talk.

"You're going to start needing bodyguards up in here," Abby tells me. "You look like hot and spicy sex on legs."

I laugh. "I'm not famous, Abby. And besides that fact, I have my family and friends here. There's no need for bodyguards."

"Well, you're famous in this bar, and I've heard your name mentioned out on the streets. Plus, I've seen the way some of these men look at you, some women, too."

"Yeah, I don't think it's come to that yet, but I like your exaggerations." I take my second shot of whiskey and swallow the warm liquid.

"Ladies and gentlemen," the MC begins, "please welcome our Friday night favorite, the alluring siren, Miss Savannah Lewis." The crowd gets loud with excitement, and I rise from my stool.

"This is for you," I say to Carter, and kiss his lips softly. Then I channel every piece of my sexy and saunter to the stage. All eyes follow me, but the only eyes I feel are Carter's.

"Savannah, Savannah, Savannah, Savannah," the entire audience chants my name continuously, along with some whistles and applause.

I take the Mic. "Thank you," I speak to the crowd.

"I love you, Savannah!" a young woman shouts.

"And I love you," I say, finding her in the crowd and smiling at her. Then I cast my eyes through the mass of my fans and say, "I love you all."

The crowd whistles, claps, and cheers.

I turn my head and give a slight nod to the band behind me, and they immediately begin to play a smooth, instrumental jazz piece. And then I start my performance, feeling the music in my bones, allowing it to provoke my words.

"Seduction," I speak into the Mic, articulating clearly, my voice sultry and silky, and the crowd becomes silent, focused on me. "Seduction is the enticement of a person and comes in many, many forms. Seduction, the way he seduced me." I take a breath.

One Night

A few whistles fill the hushed bar, hushed except for the music that's gradually swaying my hips.

I find Carter's eyes and gaze at him for a minute, and then I wink at him and continue, looking around the crowd, speaking slowly, sultry, and silky, emphasizing all the right words.

"He opened up my mouth with lust.
He filled my mouth with love.
He kissed me with a craving, with a need, with an obsession.
That kiss took me, made me moan, made me press into him harder, and made me quiver against his chiseled frame, his warm embrace.
That kiss claimed me.
He opened up my mouth with lust."

More whistles erupt from the crowd, but then fall quiet as I continue.

"Seducing me, and now I'm wanting.
Wanting
Dark, heated eyes
Undressing my body
Wanting
Skilled, expert hands
Trailing my skin
Wanting
Strong, sensual lips
Crushing my kiss
Wanting me
Making me his
And wanting more
With lustful caresses
Satisfying a raging hunger
Wanting
Filling me deep
Stretching me
Thrusting so hard
Filling me complete

Wanting
Wanting me
I am his vessel
Filling me with passion
And spilling the love
Wanting"

The bar fills with applause, hooting, and hollering, whistles mixed in, so loud, drowning out the music, which then comes to a stop. And I'm smiling at my fans, seeing Carter from the corner of my eye as he stands, grinning and clapping. And I want him. Reciting my unique and stimulating poetry has sparked a heat inside me, and the boisterous support has roused my adrenaline. And I'm wondering if Carter will actually be able to bend me over a desk, because I want him to. I need him to.

My words tonight were and are written about him. And there's more, so a hot quickie with him seems appropriate, seems right. And it's very fitting for my theme of seduction, his seduction of me.

"Thank you." I blow a kiss to my fans, then wink and wave at them, and then walk off the stage.

"That was for me?" Carter says, placing his hands on my hips and pulling me close.

I wrap my hands around his neck, staring into his eyes. "All my words tonight are for you." I kiss him, and he circles his hands around me, pulling me even closer, and then I feel the bulge in his jeans.

"Savannah!" female voices shout.

"I have to have you," Carter murmurs on my lips.

"Give me ten minutes." I kiss him, and he groans on my lips, and then releases me.

A fairly large group of young women approach me, smiling excitedly with my books in their hands. I wink at Carter with a sexy grin, and he settles back onto a barstool.

"Hi, Savannah," the ladies say.

"Hi." I smile at them. "Are you ladies having a good time?"

"Yes!" they all reply. Then one of them says, "The best time!"

"We're huge fans," another one of them says.

"The biggest," one of them adds.

I giggle at their keenness. "I love your enthusiasm, and thank you."

"I love the way you write romance, Savannah," one of the brunettes says. "I just want to jump inside your books and stay there," she adds.

"Yeah, me, too," one of the blondes agrees.

"Well, I'll tell you a little secret," I say. "Sometimes, I just want to crawl inside my stories, too."

"With a man that good looking," one of the ladies says, motioning to Carter, "you don't need to."

I turn my head and capture Carter's eyes on me, and they're heated and intense. Damn, I need to hurry up. I turn my head back to the young woman and say, "Yeah, he's special."

"You know, my boyfriend read one of your stories, because he wanted to know why I kept drooling over the men in your books," another one of the ladies says. "And now he's an animal in bed, and he brings me flowers every Monday after work."

"That's awesome," I say, smiling.

"Yeah," a brunette agrees, "that is really awesome, but I don't think I could get Johnny to read a book."

"You could always read to your man," I tell her. "My books make for a good bedtime story," I add, and wink at her.

"That's a great idea," one of the blondes says.

"Oh yeah, I'm trying that tonight," another of the ladies says, and then the entire group giggles.

"Would you ladies like me to sign your books?" I ask them.

"Oh yes, please," a couple of them say, the rest of them nodding in agreement.

"Will you take a picture with us, too?" one of the ladies asks.

"Of course," I reply.

And, one by one, I get each woman's name and sign their books, adding my positive message that is my trademark inscription. Then I take a picture with each of the ladies, and then with them as a group. And they are all ecstatic as they run to the dance floor.

"Come on, you tempting wordsmith," Carter says, taking my hand, "there's a desk around here waiting for us."

Oh hell yes!

I'm addicted to his spontaneity and impulsiveness.

As we hurry toward a hot quickie, I see Chris out of the corner of my eye. And I think he was about to approach me, but I could care less. I'm chasing an orgasm.

Carter pulls me into an office, turns on the light, and locks the door. Then he is behind me, moving my curled locks to the side, kissing my neck, and unbuttoning my shorts.

"Oh..." I moan as his fingers dip between my folds and inside my warmth.

His slides his other hand under my shirt, then travels up to my breast, and then underneath my bra, where he grabs my breast and squeezes it repeatedly, my nipple, too. And the bulge in his jeans gets harder and presses against my backside.

"Your wit makes my dick hard," he murmurs against my neck as he plants kisses all over it. I moan. "Your character makes my dick hard." He sucks on my neck and moves his fingers in and out of my accumulating wetness. I moan and moan. "Your confidence makes my dick hard." He kisses my neck and squeezes my breast. I moan. "Your words make my dick hard." He sucks on my neck, circling his fingers around my walls. I moan and moan. "Your beauty makes my dick hard." He kisses my neck and squeezes my nipple. I moan. "Your body makes my dick hard." He bites my earlobe, and I moan. "Everything about you makes me so hard," he whispers in my ear.

"Oh, Carter," I breathe. "Oh..." I moan.

Then he withdraws his fingers and releases my breast, and then he pulls down my shorts. I step one leg out of them and open up for him, spreading my legs apart.

"Bend over," he murmurs close to my ear, and I hear him unzipping his jeans.

I bend over the desk in front of me and grab the edge of it. Then he pulls my black satin thong to the side and immediately pushes his hard cock inside me, gripping my hips, and we both moan as he pulses and swells inside in my warmth and against my walls, filling me to the hilt.

"Oh god, Savannah, you feel so good," he says, his voice becoming rough as he thrusts deeply and continuously.

It's a determined, steady pace, taking my body higher and higher, building to a needed orgasm.

"Oh... Oh... Oh..." I moan and moan and moan.

"Your pussy shapes and forms around my dick so perfectly," he says, pressing his fingers into my skin. "You're mine, Savannah," he says, and thrusts even harder.

"Oh god, Carter," I breathe. "I'm... I'm... Oh..." I moan, unable to get anymore words out.

"Come for me, Gorgeous, and let me hear you," he requests.

And the beauty about our indecent and secret actions of lust is that we can be as loud as we want, because there is a rock band playing, and they are extremely booming some serious noise.

"Oh, Carter, oh, Carter," I moan and moan, managing the words out in breaths. And he begins slamming into me faster and harder, digging his fingers into my skin, gripping my hips tighter. "Oh!" I exclaim. "Carter!" I shout, and I come and come, all of my limbs vibrating.

It's so incredibly wet between us. And he keeps thrusting deeply. And I don't stop moaning.

"Your pleasure makes my dick throb," he says, his voice so very rough. "Your pleasure means everything to me," he adds. Then he bends over me and says close to my ear, "I want all of your pleasure, yours, just yours."

"Oh..." I moan, still climaxing, still vibrating.

Then he moves his hands to my backside, squeezing my ass hard, moaning and moaning, and then grunting as he fills my pussy, releasing his climax deep within.

"Fuck, Savannah," he says, stilling inside me. "You are the best drug, the best high." Then he pulls his cock slowly out of me.

He fixes my panties and helps me up. I turn around, and he kisses me, hard and possessively.

When he releases my mouth, I'm almost breathless. And we stare at one another for a minute, connecting our souls.

I clean myself up with tissues from a box on the desk and quickly put my shorts back on as Carter puts himself away back into his jeans. The band is still playing, and what we just did is between us and the four walls.

"No rehab for you," I state.

"No, none, never," he says.

"So I'm yours." I smile at him.

"You're mine, all mine," he says, and pulls me close.

"Good," I say, and kiss him. It seems that whatever he was still trying to figure out about us is being worked out nicely.

"Wear a skirt next Friday," he tells me, grinning at me with a wicked, naughty smile.

"Okay." I smile back, and then bite my bottom lip. Now I'm looking forward to next Friday already.

"Come on," he says, and takes my hand. "Let's get you back out there before people start looking for you."

We walk back to the bar and take a seat on the stools. The band is finishing up their set as Steve puts a shot of whiskey in front of me and one in front of Carter. We down our shots, the heat between us sated for now.

Steve leans into the bar. "Did you two have fun?" he asks us, his eyes smiling and his voice low-pitched, almost like a whisper.

What? How does he know?

"You two are so bad," Abby says, sitting next to me.

What the hell? I guess the walls talked. But, does everybody know?

"You know?" Carter questions Steve.

"I saw you two sneak off," he says.

"Yeah, we both did," Abby adds.

"Does anyone else know?" I ask, just a little bummed that's it's not a secret between me and Carter.

"Nobody else saw you," Steve assures us.

"Good," Carter says.

But then it dawns on me that Chris watched us sneak away. Oh well, he's not a threat and no one that I'm concerned about.

Steve places another shot of whiskey in front of each of us, plus he puts one in front of Abby, and he pours one for himself as well. "To Savannah," he begins, and raises his shot glass, "and her erotic words that make us all want to do what you two just did."

"Cheers," Abby says, raising her shot.

"I can definitely cheer to that," Carter says, and raises his shot, too.

I raise my shot glass, and we all clink ours together. "Thanks." I giggle and smile. Then we all tip our heads back and swallow our shot.

And we all converse with each other for several minutes.

One Night

"Ladies and gentlemen," the MC begins, "please welcome back the stimulating, the intriguing, the ever so sexy, Miss Savannah Lewis." The crowd claps, cheers, and whistles, and all very loudly as I rise from my position on the stool. I kiss my man on his lips, a nice and juicy one, and he grabs a big handful of my backside, squeezing it hard as our lips heat. But I recover myself quickly, and then I sexily sashay onto the stage. The crowd's noise echoes off of every wall, and I'm smiling from ear to ear.

I grab the Mic, wink at Carter and blow him a kiss, cue the band behind me, and then stare out into the packed audience. The smooth, instrumental jazz fills all of our ears. The music resonates inside me, and I feel the rhythms all over me and pushing deeper inside as I begin.

"Seduction," I speak into the Mic, slowly and in an irresistible tone, my eyes moving from face to face. "He seduced me. He lured me in." A few whistles cut through the silent mass. "Seducing me with lust," I speak, rolling the words off my tongue so sensually. "Lust, a very strong sexual desire," I speak, my voice thick with influence. "Desire, a strong feeling of wanting to have something or wishing for something to happen," I slowly speak, breaking down the definition of his seduction over me. And a few more whistles fill the air.

"Seduction, the way he seduced me. The lust, the desire, becoming so wanting," I speak into the Mic, the music controlling my body, moving me gradually but provocatively. "Wanting, in need of..." I pause, feeling Carter's heat inside me. I take a breath. "Pleasure," I speak, my mouth curling erotically with the word.

Whistling mixes with the music. "I love you, Savannah!" a guy shouts from his seat. I wink in his direction, and then continue.

"Pleasure
Lick my body
Make me quiver
Pleasure
From my neck
To my bodice
Pleasure
In-between my legs
Fervently deliver

Pleasure
Spread my thighs
Inhale my scent
Pleasure
Lick my slit
Suck on my clit
Pleasure
Push your fingers in
Circle them around
Pleasure
He's going down
Giving me so much pleasure"

My fans stand, hooting, hollering, cheering, whistling, and clapping, giving me their praise, giving me their love.

"Thank you," I speak into the Mic. I wink at my faithful following and blow them a kiss. Then I walk off the stage, and I'm immediately surrounded by animated and eager fans, both women and men, young adults and older.

I take my time, getting casual with my fans, speaking to everyone. I answer their questions. I give out sexy suggestions. I even banter with some of the guys and give some of the ladies advice, all in good, sexual fun. I sign everyone's books. I take pictures with them. And I get a few hugs from some very appreciative homemakers. Then I'm left to finally take a breath.

My eyes lock on Carter, who's standing and staring at me, watching me, drinking me in. Damn, I can already feel the charged electricity between us. The air is starting to crackle.

But I'm halted by a firm hand at the small of my back, and a cold feeling surrounds me now.

"Savannah," Chris says, lowering his hand, the tips of his fingers touching my backside and pressing into it.

I rapidly turn and face him, and his hand falls, no longer touching me. "Don't touch me," I sternly say, narrowing my eyes at him.

"What?" He brings his hand to my face in a caress, causing an icy shiver to run through me and leaving my cheek cold. "I've touched you everywhere," he says, then begins caressing my arms.

"Stop," I harshly voice, taking two steps back, out of his reach. What the hell has gotten into him?

"Why? I miss you. I want you back." His eyes are serious, and the cold is increasing with ice.

"There's nothing to have back. We were friends with benefits, and it's over. It's been over for months."

"Well, I want the benefits back." He reaches for me, and I take another step back.

"No." I shake my head. "My heart is taken, and I'm in love with someone."

His eyes cut to Carter, and Carter begins to quickly walk our way, the hot and cold colliding all around me.

"Just leave me alone, Chris." I turn and take quick steps to Carter before these two have a chance to go at it.

"Who is that?" Carter asks me, his voice sounding highly irritated and his eyes burning with exasperation.

Chris hasn't moved an inch. He's rooted in place, staring at us with great displeasure and fuming with anger.

"He's nobody. Let's just go."

But Carter doesn't move.

"His hands were all over you, and he's eyeballing the fuck out of me and you. I want to punch him in the face. Who is he?" His voice is becoming more maddened, and I begin to feel his anger increasing and exuding off of him.

"Please just get me out of here," I urge, staring into his eyes, searching them for solace.

"You're mine." He takes my hands in his and brings them to his lips, kissing each one. "And he wants what's mine. Who is he?" He keeps my hands in his and lowers them in front of our close proximity, but his anger still fills the air.

"You're jealous," I accuse him, smiling on the inside, trying to conceal it on my face.

"I'm a very jealous man," he admits, tightening his grip on my hands.

"That's kind of hot." Now I give him a smile, an arousing smile.

"Savannah, I need you to tell me who he is before I go over there and rearrange his face."

Damn, his infuriation is kind of hot, too.

I sigh with resolve. "He's an ex-friend who sort of knows me on an intimate level."

"So he was your fuck buddy, you two were friends with benefits."

"Yes," I reply, but I can see all of the unasked questions that he has. It's apparent in his eyes. "I'll explain more; just get me out of here."

Carter stares into my eyes, releases my hands, but then grabs my waist and pulls me against him. He kisses me hard. His lips are possessive, definitely showing Chris who I belong to.

And after that dominating kiss, that claiming kiss, he takes my hand and leads me out of the bar, neither one of us looking back at all. We get into a cab, on our way to Carter's loft. And as the cab drives through the streets, I tell Carter the complete story of me and Chris.

"I ended our friendship about four months ago," I say, finishing the non-romantic tale.

"Because you had zero passion for him," he states, his irritation and anger, all of his exasperation dissipating.

"Yes," I agree. "I'm obsessed with your passion." I climb onto his lap, facing him, staring into his eyes, and place my hands around his neck.

"Obsessed, possessed, and addicted," he says, voicing his feelings for me, gripping my ass in his skilled and strong hands, our heat now filling the cab. "You're mine, and I'm not letting you go." He kisses me, owning me with his lips and his tongue, all while squeezing my ass cheeks over and over.

We continue in one another's arms the rest of the way.

Then we can't get each other's clothes off fast enough, gripping, clawing, and pulling at one another's attire, all the way up to his bed, like starved animals.

"My Savannah," he whispers in my ear, and then pushes his cock inside me, filling me with one hard thrust. And it causes me to quiver and moan underneath him.

"My Carter," I murmur, gazing into his eyes.

Then his mouth is on mine as he thrusts deep and hard, taking us both to ecstasy, where we stay all night.

Chapter Fourteen

"Something smells wonderful," Carter says, coming up behind me and wrapping his arms around my waist, as I stand in front of the stove cooking our brunch. He kisses my neck.

We slept in late, very late. It's getting closer and closer to lunchtime, and we're just getting started for the day. And that's because of all the orgasms that we shared last night, all night, over and over. We both proclaimed our feelings for one another without any spoken words, but with our eyes, our touches, our mouths, and our continuous love making. It was truly special.

Carter moves a hand under my t-shirt, moves my thong to the side, and dips two fingers inside me. "You're still wet," he says at my ear. I bite my bottom lip and suppress a moan. I slept in a puddle. I woke up in a puddle. And I can't stop thinking about all those puddles he caused my body to saturate the sheets with. He moves his fingers in and out, in again, and then withdraws them. "You smell like our sex. You taste like our sex." He fixes my thong. "More sex," he whispers in my ear.

I turn off the burner and turn in his arms, wrapping my hands around his neck. "I need fuel first." I kiss his lips softly.

"What are we eating?" He smiles.

"Caprese Stuffed Avocado, mini BLT's, and eggs, sunny side up," I tell him.

"That sounds good." He squeezes my backside, kisses my lips, and then releases me.

I finish making our brunch, and then assemble our plates.

We sit at the island together and begin consuming our meal.

"This is delicious, my Savannah," he says, and gives me a knowing grin and winks at me.

I smile at him. He murmured and whispered "my Savannah" all throughout our love making last night, in my ear and while gazing into my eyes. It's hot what a little jealousy will do to a man.

"Thank you," he adds.

"You're welcome, my Carter." I may have whispered "my Carter" a few times last night as well.

Last night brought us even closer, and I fell in love with him even more, harder, but I haven't said the words out loud to him yet. He hasn't uttered the words to me either, but I know he feels it, too. The words have been exchanged between us in so many ways without speaking them, and I really like the way that we communicate our love for one another. I have no complaints.

Actions speak louder than words anyways, and our actions are definitely loud.

"What was your favorite thing to do as a child?" he asks me, sticking his fork into his eggs.

"Roller skating," I quickly reply with a smile. "My dad took me roller skating every Thursday night, just the two of us. He told my mom when she was pregnant with Lacy that he would be the first man in his daughter's life and her first date. And he kept those promises, every Thursday taking me roller skating and every Friday taking Lacy bowling."

He smiles at me. "I bet you're good on wheels."

"I am, and my dad still takes me every once in a while, so I haven't lost my touch. I'm not rusty at all."

"Good. Then I'm taking you roller skating tonight."

"Are you any good on wheels?"

"Maybe not as good as you, but I'm sure I can keep up."

"Good." I smile, and then dig into my avocado.

"So, how is your novel coming along? How many chapters do you have left to write?"

"Three," I respond. "And I'm excited. It's coming together just as I hoped for."

"I'm excited for you, too. That's a great accomplishment, and I can't wait to read it."

"If you want, you can read it once I'm done editing it."

"I would love to," he says. "And I'm still buying it as soon as it's available," he adds, and picks up his mini BLT.

"You've already bought all my books. You don't have to buy this one, too." I pick up my water and pause with it near my lips. "By the way, when did you do that?" I ask, and then take a drink.

When I woke up today, I noticed that Carter has all of my published work, sitting on the top of his bookcase that's in his bedroom. It was a surprise and instantly brought a smile to my face, but I don't remember seeing them before. And I'm usually always in his bed more than we are in mine, so I have no idea when he bought them.

"They all arrived yesterday afternoon." He picks up his coffee and takes a few sips.

"You ordered them off Amazon?"

"I did," he says.

"You didn't have to do that."

"I wanted to." He smiles at me. "I love the way you speak, and I love the words you choose, so I know your stories are great. I had to have them."

"Thank you." I smile sweetly. His little speech is flattering, and I'm humbled by it.

"Caleb also bought all of them for Ashley, and together, we bought them all for our mom, too."

"Oh my god, I don't know what to say."

"You don't need to say anything. You're amazing, and everyone should be reading your books. Now finish up. I have something I want to show you."

Damn, more surprises from my mysterious man. I could get used to this.

We finish our meal, and then he takes me up to his bedroom, where he opens up his closet and carefully pulls out a nice size framed piece of artwork.

"I've been working on this for a couple of weeks, and I want you to have it." He turns the artwork around for me to see it.

I gasp. "It's so beautiful. Oh my god, Carter, it's sexy, it's brilliant."

"It's how I see you," he says.

Carter has painted me. It's me, fully nude, lying seductively on my side on a bed that's covered in red sheets with a notebook and pen at my fingertips. My chestnut locks are flowing all over and the look in my eyes is coquettish, just like the set of my lips. It's so astounding. I can't believe he did this for me.

He hands me the painting, and I take a closer look. There's an inscription on it that says, "Painting is silent poetry and poetry is painting that speaks." It's perfect, utterly perfect.

"You captured every single detail of my face and the rest of my body," I notice. I'm in total awe of this painting and of my man, and my voice matches exactly how I feel.

"Every single curve of your body ingrained in my memory," he says slowly, his eyes darkening, repeating what he said to me the night he came back into my life.

Damn, I'm already dripping.

I carefully set the painting down, give Carter a juicy kiss, and then I drop to my knees, pulling his boxers down with me. I immediately grab his growing erection and begin sucking him into my mouth.

He moans loudly and twitches in my warm, wet control. Then he pulls his t-shirt over his head and places his hands on my face, caressing it, his fingers inching into my hair.

I take him in and out, my lips tightly suctioned around him. But then I stop quickly, pull my t-shirt over my head, exposing my breasts, my nipples, and then resume back to sucking him in and out.

My tits are bouncing a bit as I suck and suck. "Oh fuck, you are so hot," he says, his voice becoming husky, his breathing becoming rough.

But I can get hotter, and I want to. So with my free hand, I maneuver my thong off, still sucking him in and out. Then I look up at him and bring it to his nose, and I keep my sucking pace as I watch him inhale.

Damn, now I'm dripping between my thighs.

"So fucking good," he states very huskily.

I drop my thong and grab his balls. I squeeze them over and over as my mouth makes him harder and harder.

He's moaning, and our eyes are locked. I'm not the only one that's hot. He's hot, too, and so is how we are fused together.

His moans are so sexy, and I can't help but moan as well, all over his cock.

"Oh, Savannah," he murmurs. "Fuck," he breathes. He throbs in my hand, in my sucking lips, and throbs again, spilling his nut, filling my mouth.

I swallow all of him, squeezing out every last drop.

"You have a nice way of showing your gratitude. That's the best thank you I've ever received," he says, grinning from ear to ear. Then he pulls me back up, so that I'm standing, nose to nose with him, only an inch or two separating us.

"A simple thank you wasn't good enough," I say, staring into his eyes, eyes still dark with lust.

He kisses me, his tongue entering my mouth, tasting me, tasting himself. I moan into the kiss, and he lowers us to the bed. He spreads my legs apart with his knee. Then his lips are sucking all over my body as he gradually scoots down to my sex.

He grabs my thighs and inhales my scent, running his nose all over and through my pussy. I let out a loud moan and drip onto his white cotton sheets.

Then he looks up at me. "I want you to spill all over my bed and in my mouth and show me just how pleased you are." Then he scoots back up my body and says, right at my ear, "Give me your orgasm." I drip some more onto his sheets. He moves to my other ear and says, "Give me your pleasure." And I drip even more. Then he scoots back down to my sex and begins tasting me.

"Oh, Carter," I breathe, and thread my fingers through his hair, gently tugging through the caramel.

He's licking me, tasting me, loving my wet folds, loving my throbbing clit, and I can't stop moaning or watching.

Oh shit! He starts moaning, too, all over my sex.

"So good," he growls, licking, tasting, and loving.

Oh fuck. He wants my orgasm. He wants my pleasure. And it's all rapidly approaching.

But he pauses, looks up at me, pushes my bent legs farther into me, opening me up even more to him, and says, "I can taste how I've been inside you all night."

Oh shit. I bite my bottom lip, staring into his eyes, still tugging his hair, but release my lip quickly because I'm panting so much.

He grabs my ass cheeks hard, drops his head back down, licks through my slit, and then looks back up at me. "Your cream and my nut taste so fucking good together," he notes. Then he lowers his head again, squeezing my backside continuously, and devours my sex, licking and sucking every inch of it.

My whole body quivers with a huge ripple of pleasure, and I move my hands to my thighs, gripping them against me securely, helping, holding myself wide open for his oral assault. Then his tongue and his mouth get even fiercer.

I moan so extremely loud and throw my head back. "Oh, Carter, oh," I voice through my heavy panting, and press my fingers into my thighs.

Never have I ever been with a man before that's been concerned with wanting my orgasms and wanting my pleasure. And never do I ever want to give them to anyone else.

My inner vixen, who's been naked, moaning, panting, and writhing in pleasure since last night, is nodding in agreement as she soils her sheets yet again.

Carter's mouth is so ravenous on my sex, and his moans exhibit his hunger. And I'm ready to feed him.

Pleasure consumes me, spreading through me entirely, making me vibrate and making me spill a puddle. "Carter, oh, Carter, oh, Carter," I loudly say, giving him my orgasm, my orgasm coated in so much pleasure.

He licks me and sucks on me until my fluids stop pouring out and my body relaxes.

And as I release my thighs, Carter is entering my pussy, pushing his cock in all the way.

"Oh..." I moan. "My Carter, my cock," I say, gazing into his eyes and wrapping my hands around his neck.

He begins to thrust in and out. "Your words, my Savannah," he says, then presses his lips to mine, kissing me with belonging.

His bedroom is an inferno, and we are the flames, burning in passion, burning in love.

"I need to be deeper in my pussy," he says, his voice husky, and he pushes my bent legs against my body once again. Then I grab them and hold them, and he thrusts, filling every wet inch of my insides and more.

I am so open for this man, wide fucking open, and I can't stop watching his cock move in and out of me. It's such a hot sight, and my folds are fluttering with his every thrust. Damn, I'm barely blinking.

"Oh, Savannah, you are so sexy," he says, pushing his cock in deeper than deep. "And it's even sexier watching you watch me claim my pussy." He starts thrusting harder, and his balls smack me near my anus over and over.

His cock is so thick, so hard, and so wet with my climax and added arousal. It slides in, disappearing in its domain. It reappears, glistening and pulsing. In and out, I bite my bottom lip, mesmerized by its magnificence, by its ability, by the complete feeling as it occupies and declares its residence. His cock is the best, ever.

Our moans fill the loft. Our heavy breathing bounces off all the walls. Our potent aroma wafts through the air. Our passion transfers back and forth between each other. It mixes together. It takes us to ecstasy. Our sex is the best, ever.

Damn, his cock, his remarkable cock, my cock... In and out, it's so tight, getting tighter and tighter. The feelings, the fullness, the visuals, it's all so intense. God, I'm ready to watch myself come.

And I do, and so does he.

"Oh! Oh! Oh! Oh! Oh!" I shout my moans as I climax and release all over, my pussy fluttering and fluttering, my legs vibrating in my grip.

"Oh fuck, that is so hot. You are so hot," he says, his voice very husky, his cock still thrusting in and out.

My orgasm flows out of me like a river. It's everywhere, all over him and a puddle beneath me. And it's still flowing.

Carter dips a couple fingers in my sticky flow. He brings them to his mouth and sucks them clean. Then he dips them in my flow again, but brings them to my mouth. I open and suck them clean, my eyes clouded by my orgasm but locked with his. And my flavor tastes of my pleasure.

"You are so perfect," he says, taking my hands in his, threading his fingers through, and placing our entwined hands above my head as he gradually collapses on top of me.

My legs go slack, falling open at our sides, and he continues to fill me deep, moving in and out of my excessive wetness.

"So perfect," he murmurs, then makes love to my mouth.

He kisses me affectionately, his lips warm and tender, his tongue leading in a slow dance. It matches the stroke of his cock now, and my whole body hums in love.

The last of my long, extraordinary orgasm wets his groin, making it very damp between us, and then he climaxes, throbbing and throbbing as he releases inside me. And every time our thick cream blends and combines, more of our hearts open up and issue more of our love story.

His cock owns me, and his tongue has sealed the deal. I am undoubtedly his.

"Mine," he whispers in my ear.

Yes, his.

He kisses my lips softly, and then withdraws from my sex. He lies on his back and pulls me into him, hugging me to his side. And our breathing begins to even out as we relax in a sated afterglow.

"How about we rest for a little, and then I'll run us a bath?" he says, caressing my back.

"Yeah, I like that idea."

He kisses my forehead, and then my eyes close.

*   *   *   *   *   *   *   *

"These are great burgers," I voice. "The right amount of grease and cheese," I add.

Carter and I are having dinner at a nearby hamburger joint. It's just a small hole-in-the-wall restaurant, but the food is delicious. We both got cheeseburgers with fries and coleslaw, his burger loaded with a lot more extras than mine. Everything is made fresh every day, and I can't believe that I've never been here before.

"They are really good," he agrees.

After our wet and sticky afternoon and our short snooze, we took a bath together. Our muscles throughout our bodies and our sexual muscles were soothed. Our oversexed bodies were cleaned. And we were refreshed. And then the heavily soiled sheets on his bed were changed. Then we channeled our sexy artistry and each did a little work, me writing in a notebook and him sketching in his fairly big sketchbook. We had a great afternoon, and now we're embarking on a fun evening.

"What's your favorite movie?" he asks me, and then takes a drink of his beer, a Miller straight from the bottle.

"Dirty Dancing," I reply. "When I was a young kid, my mom got Lacy and I hooked on the movie and we used to get in front of my parents' big full-length mirror and try to copy all of Jennifer Grey's moves."

He chuckles. "I bet that was cute."

"It was definitely funny." I take a drink of my beer, and Carter eats a few fries. "My parents shared some laughs and thought we were cute, but they put on the real show. They would reenact the dances between Patrick Swayze and Cynthia Rhodes and, of course, the ones between Patrick Swayze and Jennifer Grey."

"Your parents are so into each other and so in love. I bet they were great, maybe even sexier than the actors."

"They made it look effortless, that's for sure." I smile. Then I eat the last of my burger.

"I was fighting pirates while you were dancing in front of the mirror," he says with a grin.

"Peter Pan?" I take a guess.

"Yeah," he nods with a slight chuckle. "Caleb and I would play with other boys in our neighborhood and act like the lost boys and pirates."

"Didn't everyone want to be Peter Pan?"

"Yeah, him and Captain Hook," he says. "We had a few fights over it, and those fights would sometimes work their way into us play fighting. Caleb and I got a few scrapes and bruises, along with the other kids, too. Then we finally got smart and decided to all take turns being those characters."

I giggle. "That's really funny, but all your moms probably didn't think so."

"My mom just always said, "Boys will be boys." And my dad would even show me and Caleb fighting techniques."

"Your parents are cool." I smile.

"Yeah, but maybe not as cool as yours," he says.

"My parents are definitely in a league of their own."

"I think you classify in a league of your own, too," he says, grinning. "Now let's finish up, so you can show me just how good you are on wheels. I bet you do that sexy, too."

"Maybe," I say, and wink at him, and his smile broadens.

We finish our dinner and take a cab to the roller skating rink, where the music is loud and energetic, the people are happy and lively, and colorful lights are flashing all over. We're both ready for a good time and immediately get our skates, old school skates with four wheels on each skate. Then we roll onto the hard yet smooth floor and let the music take us around.

The music is a good mix of all of today's hits, mainly fast, popular tunes in the rock, pop, and rap genres, and I show Carter exactly how capable I am on wheels. I get a bouncing groove in me, swaying my hips, using hand movements, and criss-crossing my feet to the beats. And he does a decent job by my side, not as groovy as me, but he keeps up with me as we circle and loop the rink over and over.

We're having a great time, both of us smiling and laughing, and he spins me around a few times, adding to our enthusiasm.

We continue like this for a few songs, and then I get really sexy on my wheels, bouncing into the beats even more rhythmically with every glide.

I have the dancing and skating technique working for me. Carter is impressed and really enjoying watching me move. He's trailing behind me and whistling quietly. It makes me want to shake my ass for him, so I do, just a little.

"So sexy," he says close to my ear, and then smacks my backside, making my smile widen. Then he speeds up in front of me and turns around, so that he's skating backwards, his eyes focused intently on me. He whistles a bit louder. "Very sexy," he says, his eyes lighting up as he watches.

I have a few eyes on me from other skaters as well, but Carter is the only one making a big deal about it. And I'm enjoying his reactions.

And after a really sexy song, Sexy Dirty Love by Demi Lovato, and me displaying just how sexy it makes me feel, Carter is back at my side and holding my hand quite possessively. I guess he needs everyone to know that all my sexy belongs to him. And honestly, it turns me on.

Then after a while, the songs slow down, sexy but slow, and we skate, hand in hand, for the rest of our loops around the rink.

"Thank you for such a fun evening," I tell Carter as he's hailing us a cab.

"Thank you for entertaining me with your skating abilities," he says as a cab pulls up to the curb. "You're sexy in everything that you do, and I love it," he adds, opening the car door for me.

I slide into the cab, Carter following after me, and then he gives the driver my address.

"We're going back to my place?" I say quizzically, because I rather like making his sheets wet.

"Yes," he says with a mischievous look in his eyes. "I want to dig around in your box of toys."

"Ooh," I purr, and pick up his hand. "My Carter has sticky fingers." I take his index finger into my mouth, slowly suck on it, my eyes locked with his, and then I remove it. "What will his sticky fingers adhere to?" I take his middle finger into my mouth and slowly suck.

"You're making my dick hard," he says, his voice low yet deep, so sexy in its natural tone.

"Good." I smile and release his hand.

"My Savannah, the epitome of sexy and so naughty," he says, and then kisses me with his lustful tongue.

*   *   *   *   *   *   *   *

In my bedroom, I begin stripping off my clothes as Carter's hands are buried in my box of toys. Then he shows me what he has chosen. He's going a very kinky route, and my body instantly tingles in anticipation, especially my nipples.

I lick my lips as I stare at the three items in his hands. "I'm glad the lube is present," I tell him. "My ass wants the attention of your cock."

He sets the items on my bed at the edge of it, where I wait, and then he pulls his graphic t-shirt over his head. "Your ass is on the same page as me and my dick," he says, his eyes getting darker as he unzips his jeans.

"Mm," I lick my bottom lip and bite it as he exposes what me and my ass wants.

"You look hungry for me," he says, hooking his hand around my waist, scooting us up my bed as he lowers himself on top of me.

"Very," I say, slipping my hands around his neck and gazing into his eyes. "You look hungry, too."

"Ravenous," he says, then drops his lips to mine, kissing me breathless.

And then he doesn't waste any time feeding our famished desires.

And I'm still trying to catch my breath as he grabs the first kinky item.

My nipple clamps, I love my nipple clamps. I love the bite and the sting of them every time I pull on the chain. It sends a rush of hot pleasure through my entire body. And they're the soft rubber kind, so I don't feel any pain, just a fucking good time.

Carter attaches them to my nipples and gently tugs on the chain, making me smile and my body buzz with the thrill. "So hot," he says, "you and your tits, so hot."

Then he grabs the next kinky item, turns it on, and promptly begins gliding it all over me as I pull on the chain and delight in the sensations my nipples are receiving.

My wand, I call it "My Magic Wand." It is the best vibrator, even though it only stimulates my exterior body, my skin and sometimes my clit. But it does the best job without even entering me. It makes me wet. It makes me come. It makes me scream. What it does to my body is exactly the same thing that Carter does to me with his touch. The touch of his hands and the touch of his mouth, I should start calling him "My Magic Wand." His touch is magic.

He slowly glides my wand over my tingling skin as he stares into my eyes, and I tug on the nipple clamp chain repeatedly, showing him my pleasure through my impassioned gaze.

"Gorgeous," he says, moving the wand along every inch of my skin, making me wet, very wet, making me vocal, very vocal.

I'm moaning loudly. I'm tugging. I'm dripping. I'm quivering. I am all consumed by his kinky choices as he's in-between my legs bringing me to orgasmic heights.

He brings the wand over my clit and inserts two fingers inside my sex. He circles his fingers around and lightly brushes my clit with the fast and powerful vibrations. And then I'm coming. I'm coming hard, spilling everywhere, quivering all over, and screaming my moans, my eyes wide open and still gazing into his.

But he quickly removes his fingers, only touching my insides for a few hot seconds. "So warm, so wet," he says, licking his sticky fingers.

I continue to come, to shake, to tug, to moan, to be in the heart of my orgasm.

And then he pushes his rock-solid cock inside me, filling me full and stilling. He moves the wand to my breasts and takes the chain from me. He pulls on the chain and circles the wand around, but he's still unmoving inside me. And it doesn't matter, my sex responds anyway.

My inner walls grab him and hold him, squeezing him continuously, giving him good reason to be buried inside me and motionless, and he smiles at me.

"So warm, so wet, and so tight," he says, bringing me to another round of orgasmic heights with the constant attention to my breasts and nipples.

I want his thrusts, but I know that he's saving them for my ass. So I grip the sheets and begin thrusting my pussy, making the hard hitting movements myself.

"You're going to make me come," he says, his voice a little rough.

"Then come with me," I say, my voice very, very breathy as I'm ready to spill again.

I'm moaning loudly and thrusting hard, and then I come even louder and harder.

"Oh fuck," he voices. He drops the wand, removes the nipple clamps, and then lowers his body on me. He takes over and starts thrusting in me deep and hard.

"Oh, Carter, oh yes!" I exclaim as my orgasm continues.

"Oh, Savannah, I'm coming," he murmurs, his hands in my hair as his cock throbs against my tight and squeezing hold.

We're both coming, our orgasms mixing together, and we stare into each other's eyes, watching pleasure exude from our gaze.

God, my nipple clamps and my wand are much more intense with another person involved. I love when he uses my toys on me.

But I love his cock even more.

Once our bodies calm down, he grabs the lube. Then he strokes himself and watches my afterglow.

"You are so beautiful, so sexy," he says, "such a gorgeous woman."

"And all yours," I add. "Now fuck me again."

"Still very hungry," he says, grinning.

"Yes, and you're able to come and usually squeeze another one out, so squeeze another one out inside my ass."

He chuckles. "My Savannah and that dirty and erotic mouth... So perfect," he says. Then he begins rubbing lube all around my anus and all over his sticky cock.

I grab his cock as he tosses the lube aside, and I guide him into my ass.

"Shit," he voices as I continue pushing him inside me.

"So tight, so good," I murmur, talking like him now.

"You are so perfect," he says, covering me with his hard, muscular body, his cock fully in me. He thrusts in me once, and then stills. "You are the only one that I've ever stayed hard for." He thrusts in me again, and then stills. "You are the only one that can make me come back-to-back."

"Oh, Carter," I breathe, and wrap my hands around his neck, pulling him to my mouth.

He takes my lips and kisses me, filling my mouth with his tongue. And then he slowly thrusts in my ass, one delicious stroke after another.

I'm on a cloud, floating in bliss. He's basically just told me that I'm the best that he's ever had, and that confession has me falling in love with him harder and deeper.

I'm living out the stuff I write about, and I can't wait to turn the page.

Chapter Fifteen

"They're on their way," Lacy says to Abby and I as she looks up from her phone.

We're dressed and waiting for our men to pick us up. They are taking us out for dinner and dancing at an establishment that offers both. The place is called Taste Listen Twirl. The food is supposed to be absolutely amazing, and the music is supposed to be a collective mix of upbeat jazz, bouncing hip hop, and funky R&B. None of us have ever been there, and we're all looking forward to it. It should be a very fun evening.

"And Caleb and Ashley are meeting us there," Lacy adds as she sets down her phone.

The three of us are sitting in our living room having a drink while we wait. We actually had time to spare after we completed our hair, makeup, and slipped on our clothes, so we're talking and drinking red wine.

We're all wearing exceedingly nice and short, slinky and tight dresses, so hopefully, we don't spill any wine. Abby is looking beautiful and bright in a light yellow strappy cami dress. Lacy is looking sinfully sexy in a peach off the shoulder irregular dress. And I'm looking phenomenal in a red curved hem dress. We're all showcasing some serious legs with open-toe strappy high heels adorning our feet, each of us in different shades, Abby with white heels, Lacy with a nude color heel, and me with red heels. We all look great, extremely hot and sexy.

"Brian has an SUV, right?" Abby says.

"Yes," Lacy says, "and it's big and spacious, plenty of room for the six of us."

Brian, unlike all of us, lives right outside of the city in a nice and quiet suburb, but he works in the city, so he owns a vehicle. He works in finance. He's a bank manager at one of the most prestigious and biggest financial chains in all of the Midwest. Lacy's never dated such a prominent man before. She really scored with him, and he is quite perfect for her.

But Abby's really scored with her man, too. Not only is Steve a bartender at the hottest bar in Chicago and all of Illinois, but he's also in school getting his master's degree in business. He plans on running the entire bar soon, and the owner is already grooming him for it. And Abby lets her teacher side out occasionally with him and helps him study. They're so cute together.

And Carter has brightened my world as well. It's been six weeks now since he's came back into my life, and I fall in love more and more every day. I know I can say the same for him, too. He has said the words in his dreams, always after murmuring my name. I know I've said the words in my dreams, too. I woke up the other night as his name and those three words escaped my lips, and Carter was instantly all over me, loving me in every way, so I'm pretty sure that's what woke him up as well. And his response showed me just how much he loves me, too. I'm the happiest I've ever been.

"Love is in the air tonight," Abby says, smiling brightly.

"It sure is," Lacy agrees with the same bright smile.

"Love
It circles us and enfolds us
Sparking flame after flame
The heat consuming us
The passion owning us
Love
Present in our eyes
Sealed upon our lips
Transferred with every kiss
Spread thick with every touch
Love
Taking us home

Two hearts locked together
Exchanging the keys
Permanently one another's property
Love
True
Deep
Hard
Never letting go
Love"

"That's beautiful," Abby says with a twinkling shine in her eyes.

"It's hot, too, Little Vixen," Lacy says, and winks at me, then raises her wine glass. "Cheers, to love."

"Cheers," Abby and I say, raising our wine glasses and all three of us lightly tapping them together.

We finish our wine, and right on cue, there's a knock on the door. Lacy gets up and answers it, and our apartment is immediately filled with undeniable striking masculinity as the boys come walking inside. They look great.

They greet us all, smiling. Then Steve personalizes his greeting for Abby, complementing her beauty and kissing her. Brian personalizes his greeting for Lacy, appreciating her sex appeal and kissing her. And Carter personalizes his greeting for me, circling me in his arms, telling me I'm stunningly gorgeous, and then kissing me.

Mm, he smells so good, like vanilla with spice.

And they all clean up very nice. Steve is wearing dark navy dress pants, a white collar button-down shirt with the top button undone, and brown dress shoes. Brian is wearing gray dress pants, a white collar button-down shirt with a purple tie, and black dress shoes. Carter is wearing black dress pants, a royal blue collar button-down shirt that accentuates his eyes and with the top two buttons undone, and black dress shoes. We definitely have some hot dates tonight.

"You all look very beautiful," Brian says. "Are you ladies ready?" he asks.

"Yes," Lacy replies, smiling. Abby and I smile our answer as our men take our hands in theirs.

Carter threads his fingers through mine and leads me out the door, and I lock it as we're the last ones out. Then we all gather into Brian's SUV, and he drives us to the posh restaurant/club.

* * * * * * * *

"How is everything?" our blonde haired waitress asks as she supplies us with another bottle of wine.

"Everything is wonderful," Brian says with a grin.

"It's excellent," Caleb adds, grinning as well.

We have an assortment of delectable food dishes at our table, and we all are enjoying portions of everything. Each one of the dishes is big, each being enough for a few servings. There is grilled blackened salmon on a bed of wild rice with sautéed asparagus. There is shrimp scampi. There is butternut squash ravioli with seared chicken. There is fillet mignon over mashed potatoes and gravy with sliced, sautéed carrots. And the wine keeps flowing.

The food is mouth-watering. The music is dynamic and very catchy, foot-tapping, bouncing in your seat good fun. The entire place is vibrant and filled with much exuberance. It's a superb time being had by all eight of us.

"Savannah, I'm really enjoying your books," Ashley tells me with a big smile on her face.

"We both are," Caleb says, and then kisses his wife's cheek, which is now blushing with a light shade of red.

I quietly giggle at his comment.

Ashley clears her throat, her blush fading to pink. "I just love your poetry, too," she says. "Can you just come up with poems right on the spot?"

I smile at her and set down my wine.

"Love
It fills my heart
I think it has from the very start
Love
It follows me in my dreams
It works its way into every thought
Love

It stalks me
It owns me
Love
Every look
Every touch
Every kiss
It desires to win
Love
It resides deep within"

"I love that," Ashley says, her whole face lit up. "I'm going to need your signature on all of my copies of your books, because you're going places, girl."

Everyone is grinning at me, their lips curled in enjoyment and admiration, plus their eyes smiling at me.

"I'm already on my way." I smile at her and wink.

"I love your confidence, too," she says.

"Me, too," Abby agrees. "Both of the Lewis sisters," she adds.

Lacy smiles and says, "Confidence is the key to being sexy, and everyone at this table is sexy, so let's go spread our confidence out on the dance floor."

"Come on, Sexy," Brian says, standing and offering Lacy his hand.

"Shall we, my Love," Caleb says, standing and offering Ashley his hand.

Carter leans in real close, his fingers brushing against my nape and his other fingers trailing along my thigh. "Love," he murmurs in my ear, "from the very start." He licks my earlobe. Damn, his fingers and tongue dampen my panties and awake my inner vixen, who then stretches with an inviting smile taking over her mouth. "Me, too, Savannah," he murmurs in my ear, "from the very start." He sucks my earlobe.

I turn my head and lock with his gaze. "Me, too," he repeats, brushing his fingers over my cheek, and then he kisses me. He kisses me with love, filling my mouth with it, filling my soul with it.

Love, our love...

And when he releases me, we're the only ones left at the table.

"You want to twirl me around?" I ask him.

"Yeah, let's go show them all how it's done." He stands and offers me his hand. I take it, rise, and walk with him onto the dance floor.

The music is great. It's a mix of the three genres, and the beats are unlike anything I've heard before. It's a live band with vocalists and rhymers. It's loud. It's booming. The drums resonate inside me. It's wholly enthralling.

Carter leads me with quick steps, getting groovy on his feet. He moves me around fast with the tempo, and then spins me out a few times. It's fun, and we both smile at one another as he moves us across the smooth floor.

We dance together for a while, and then eventually, Carter and all the guys go back to our table. They leave us girls to continue dancing as they square away the bill and have the remaining food boxed up, allowing each of us small portions of each dish to take home. Then they sit, chat, and sip on more wine while they watch us being confident and sexy.

I'm having a good time dancing with my girls. I'm bouncing, twirling, shaking, and twisting my body to the funk that fills my ears. It's fun, but I'm kind of in my own bubble, feeling the music, not really paying much attention to anything else. And that turns out to be a mistake.

"Savannah," Chris says close to my ear as he's behind me and grabbing my arm. I instantly feel cold, and before I can speak or respond in any way, he's turning me around. "Dance with me," he says, and begins taking me into his arms.

"No! Chris, stop!" I loudly voice, and try pushing out of his hold he has on me.

"Get your hands off her, Chris," Lacy demands.

"Shut up, Lacy," he spits out, sounding irritated. "This doesn't concern you." He grips me harder and narrows his eyes.

"You're right, Chris," she says. "It concerns her man." She hurries off the dance floor, along with Abby and Ashley, heading toward our table.

"You look better with me," Chris says, digging his fingers into my skin, piercing it with his nails. "You belong with me," he says, almost puncturing my skin, his nails feeling like tiny knives.

This isn't the Chris I know. This isn't the man that I once called a friend. He's cold. He's delusional. He's menacing. And I feel sick to my stomach.

"Let me go, Chris," I cry, tears running down my face. "You're hurting me. Please stop," I beg, my voice breaking with my sobs.

His forceful grip is bruising. His stabbing hold is cutting. His covetous rage is painful. And I can't break free.

But then familiar warmth mixes with the cold, and I'm suddenly out of Chris's angry grip.

Carter doesn't waste a single second and balls up his fists and punches Chris, connecting fast and hard with his jaw.

Chris stumbles back, but doesn't back down. "You don't deserve her," he says loud and clear.

Some of the surrounding patrons begin slowing down their movements and focus their attention on the aggressive scene that's playing out, but the music continues to beat groovy and funky.

Carter doesn't speak. He just acts. He punches Chris again, this time connecting with his nose, and blood starts to drip from Chris's nostrils.

Chris stumbles again and shouts out a slew of curses and derogatory remarks, still not backing down. He balls up his fists and charges at Carter.

But Carter is quicker. He dodges Chris's fist, and then he punches Chris again, fast and hard, directly in the nose again. And this time, Chris falls to the dance floor, shouting and blood steadily flowing from his crooked nostrils.

And Carter does not stop.

He bends down, grabs Chris's shirt by the collar, and swings blow after blow, punching Chris's face all over, causing blood to spatter.

I can feel Carter's extreme outrage, and it's a whole other thing to witness it. I've never seen this side of Carter, not once. He's consumed by fury, and I'm beginning to panic.

Chris is borderline unconscious, his eyes rolling, his eyelids sagging. And there's so much blood.

"Carter, stop, please," I implore, tears still staining my face.

But he doesn't stop.

"Carter, you're going to kill him," I cry.

Then Caleb and Brian rapidly approach and grab Carter and pull him off of Chris, and Chris groans like a wounded animal.

Caleb has Carter locked in his grip with Brian standing in front of them, not allowing Carter to attack any further.

Carter stretches his head past Brian and locks his eyes on me, and I'm instantly scared. He's breathing hard, and his eyes are full of and exuding a crazed rage. He doesn't look like himself. He looks like a monster.

"Get him out of here before the cops show up," Brian tells Caleb, his voice low.

Caleb nods and muscles Carter out the back door of the building, Ashley following behind them.

Steve begins to help Chris up, and I run to the bathroom in a hurry, where I bend in front of a toilet and proceed to vomit.

"Savannah," both Abby and Lacy call out as they enter the bathroom.

I throw up the last of my disgust, wipe my mouth, flush the toilet, and straighten back up.

"We need to get you out of here," Lacy tells me.

I nod, trying to fight back the sobs that are threatening my eyes, the sobs that are threatening my heart.

Lacy and Abby escort me out of the bathroom and out of the entire building. Steve is waiting for us at the back door and takes us to Brian's SUV. And as I'm climbing in, I faintly hear a few voices and Chris's voice coming from the ambulance that's somewhat nearby, which a couple of police officers are gathered at.

"Can you tell us what happened?" one of the officers asks Chris.

"I'm not really sure," Chris says, his voice strained from the beat down, his words slow. "It all happened really fast. I was dancing with a girl, and then I was suddenly on the floor getting hit over and over."

Steve closes the door, muffling anymore voices, and then he climbs in the passenger seat.

Brian starts driving. "He's not going to tell the cops anything. He's not pressing charges," he informs me, eyes on the road.

"How do you know?" I ask. Chris seems very intent on getting Carter out of my life in any way that he can.

"I reminded him that you are very capable of pressing domestic charges against him."

"Yeah," Lacy agrees, sitting next to me, "you're already starting to bruise."

"And he left some marks on you," Abby adds, sitting on the other side of me.

"So, he's really not going to talk?"

"No, he's not," Brian assures me.

"His whole face is swelling up fast. He's missing a tooth, and his nose is broken. I don't think he could form anymore words if he wanted to," Steve says.

"And he doesn't want to," Lacy adds.

The rest of the drive to my apartment is quiet, but my mind isn't quiet. I keep seeing Carter's rage-filled eyes, and I'm fighting back tears that are ready to take me over entirely.

*   *   *   *   *   *   *   *

"Can I get you anything?" Abby asks me, looking concerned, her love for me radiating in her eyes.

"No, I'm just going to go to bed." And I escape into my bedroom.

I take off my dress and my heels and slip on one of Carter's t-shirts that he left here and a pair of my leggings. And as I'm doing so, I take notice of my bruises and marks that are all over my arms. And my tears begin to fall down my face.

I hurry to my bed, climbing in and wrapping my comforter around me.

But I can't get warm. The warmth is gone.

The cold creeps into my room, filling the space completely, surrounding me and engulfing me in frost. And I cry myself into a troubled sleep of anguish.

Chapter Sixteen

The rain is pouring down nonstop, and I'm sitting outside allowing myself to get soaked, drenched from head to toe. But it's not soothing me. I don't think anything can at this point.

I barely slept last night. In fact, I haven't been sleeping well at all for the past few days. The look in Carter's eyes and the rage that he unleashed on Chris has been haunting me ever since, and it's been four days. I just can't stop thinking about it.

And Carter's been contacting me every day, which doesn't help me to take my mind off of it either. He called me the day after the incident, and he's been calling each day since then, plus texting me, too, but I haven't picked up or replied. I'm conflicted, and I don't know what to do.

I love him. I want to be with him. I know he would never hurt me, but seeing such a violent side of him really scared the hell out of me. I need answers, and I know he'll give them to me, but I'm not sure I'm ready to hear the truth. The truth could be the end of us, even though I can't picture my world without him.

And my world without Carter would kill my heart, and I would never be the same, never be whole.

Abby cracks open the sliding door from our living room and peeks her head out. "Savannah, please come inside," she urges.

I've been sitting in the rain for hours, and Abby has been trying to get me to come inside ever since she got home from work.

"Come on, I can tell you're freezing. Your lips are turning purple, and you're shivering."

"I like the rain," I insist.

"I know you do, but this is not you enjoying it."

I sigh. She doesn't understand. I'm not cold from the rain. I'm cold from Carter's absence.

"Come on, I made chicken noodle soup," she says. "It's homemade, and I made hot chocolate, too."

I sigh again. I guess I should eat. I've barely been doing much of that these past few days. So I get up and drag myself inside.

"Go get cleaned up," Abby tells me. "Lacy will be home in a bit, and then we can all have dinner together."

"Okay."

I enter my bedroom, grab some clean, dry clothes, and then I exit my room and disappear into the bathroom.

I don't look like myself. I look like a pale, ghostly version of myself, so I avoid the mirror. I take my wet clothes off and ring them out in the bathtub and hang them on the shower rod. I dry my body off and towel dry my hair. I put on a white cotton thong, a purple t-shirt, light gray leggings, cotton socks, and I put my robe on over everything. Then I exit the bathroom.

"Hey," Lacy says, leaving her bedroom, just getting home from my parents' store, "did you just get out of the shower?"

"No, the rain," I reply.

"Oh," she says, and we join Abby in the kitchen.

We each get a bowl of steaming, hot chicken noodle soup, a fresh and toasted baguette, and a coffee mug full of hot chocolate. Then we sit down at the table and begin eating.

"Have you gotten any writing done?" Lacy asks me.

"No." I blow on my soup, not wanting to meet her eyes.

"I'm worried about you," she says, and I can feel her eyes all over me, glued to me.

"I'm worried about you, too," Abby says, and I feel her eyes all over me as well.

"I'm fine," I lie, and continue to blow on my soup.

"No you're not," Abby says.

"Definitely not," Lacy agrees. "You're moping around here like you're going through a breakup."

I drop my spoon in my bowl and look up at them. "I don't know what to do."

"What does your heart say?" Abby asks me.

"That I've finally found what I've been waiting for," I acknowledge. I take a deep breath and blow it out. "From the moment I showed an interest in the opposite sex, I've always known what I wanted in a man, even though I've let a few assholes into my life and my bed. Carter is the chemistry, the passion, and the explosive fireworks that I've been holding out for, that I've been writing about. He's supposed to be my happily ever after."

"You need to talk to him," Lacy says.

"You didn't see the look in his eyes," I shoot back.

"I saw enough," she asserts.

"Lacy's right," Abby says. "You can't let one fucked up night destroy what you two have. You love him, and he loves you."

"We've never openly said those words to each other," I admit, and I pick my spoon back up.

"Really," Lacy says, looking surprised.

I nod. "We've expressed it in every way possible, with other words, our actions, and the physical between us, but just not those three specific words."

"Well, it's obvious that you two are in love," Abby says, smiling at me. "Talk to him."

"I know I need to. I'm just worried and nervous about what I might find out."

"He may have a skeleton or two in his closet," Lacy says, "but the way he defended you was so fucking hot."

I roll my eyes at her and eat my soup.

"Whatever. Roll your eyes if you want to, but Carter has a burning passion for you."

"I know."

"He was aggressive with raw emotion, but I have to agree," Abby says. "He reacted as a man deeply in love, and a man with intense passion is undeniably a package of red-hot excitement."

"Exactly," Lacy says, smiling.

"We're obsessed with each other's passion," I tell them.

"He is your happily ever after," Abby says, smiling.

"Just tell your mind to shut the hell up and listen to your heart," Lacy says, and winks at me.

"I'll call him." I give her a small smile.

"Tonight," she says.

I nod, and go back to eating my soup.

I can sense their smiles as I'm dipping my spoon into my chicken noodle soup, and then the conversation finally changes course.

"We just got a new toy in today," Lacy begins, but she's interrupted by the door.

"I'll get it," Abby says, rising from her seat.

"Wow!" Lacy exclaims. "Who are they for?"

I look up from my soup, and Abby is holding a beautiful crystal vase that is full of fresh, vibrant red roses, and there seems to be more than a dozen.

"It's two dozen roses for Savannah," Abby says, and sets them on the table, right in the center.

"Red roses convey deep emotions, like love, longing, and desire, but also sometimes regret and sorrow," I affirm. Damn, they're absolutely gorgeous.

"What does the card say?" Abby asks me, her whole face smiling.

I pick up the card and read it out loud.

My Savannah

You are my everything, and without you, I'm nothing. I need you. I miss you. And I'm not letting you go.

Your Carter

"Burning passion," Lacy says, smiling.

"He loves you," Abby says, smiling from ear to ear.

"And I love him." I smile at them.

*   *   *   *   *   *   *   *

I'm sitting outside again, but it's not raining anymore. The sun is setting, and there's a faint rainbow across the evening sky. It's a beautiful night.

"You are so gorgeous," a familiar deep voice says.

"Carter," I breathe, and the warmth returns, and an abundance of love fills my heart.

Chapter Seventeen

I'm sitting on the edge of my bed, and Carter is standing against the wall, staring at me, his eyes full of so many emotions.

"You scared me," I tell him.

"I know, and I'm so sorry." He looks utterly remorseful.

"Why couldn't you stop yourself?"

"Seeing that guy aggressively manhandle you brought me back to a dark time in my life. And then seeing the tears in your eyes triggered me even more, and I reacted without thinking twice."

"What's in your past? Will you tell me?"

He takes a deep breath and blows it out. "Three years ago, I was supposed to get married."

My eyes get huge in their sockets as I listen to him reveal more of his mystery.

"I caught my best friend, who was also my best man, and my fiancé having an affair."

"Oh my god," I murmur.

"I walked in on them in the actual act, just two days before my wedding."

"That's horrible," I say, shaking my head.

"I punched him. I almost knocked him out. I spit on her. Then I called off the wedding and never spoke to either of them again."

Damn, that explains his jealousy, his possessiveness, and his brutal reaction.

"And a couple months later, I was informed that she was pregnant, and that they were getting married as soon as possible."

Damn, that's so fucked up. I don't know what to say, so I continue to listen and stare into his eyes.

"I was full of so much hate and anger that I just had to get away. I needed to escape, so that's when I took off to Europe."

"But you eventually came back."

"I did, and I immersed myself into my art, painting and drawing as often as I could. And eventually over much time, I didn't want to go back to the casino. All I wanted to do was create art, so I took off to Hawaii to think about my life."

He takes a few steps and sits on the bed next to me, and the warmth around me intensifies. I let my robe fall off my shoulders as he grips my chin and turns my face toward his. And I get lost in his eyes. His eyes are radiating love, so much love.

Then he caresses my cheek. "You are the first woman I've connected with in such a long time, the first woman I've touched, the first woman I've kissed, the first woman I've taken to bed." He pauses, taking a breath and blowing it out. "I fell in love with you that night, and it scared the hell out of me."

"So you freaked out and took off."

He nods. "But thankfully, fate brought me back to you, and I fall more and more in love with you every day. I'm never letting you go, not ever."

"Good because I love you."

His eyes begin to smolder, and he takes my face in his hands. He presses his lips to mine and kisses me with so much love, passion, and intensity. He leaves me breathless.

"Lie back," he says, pulling my robe off me. I do, and he rises and pulls his black t-shirt over his head.

Damn, I bite my bottom lip. I will never get tired of looking at him. Clothed or unclothed, he is a gorgeous man, hard, strong, and chiseled to perfection.

Carter holds my gaze and slowly begins undressing me. He pulls my leggings down and disrobes me of them and my socks. Then he unbuttons and unzips his jeans and pulls them down, along with his boxer briefs, and out springs his hard, thick erection. I bite my bottom lip again.

He climbs on the bed, fully nude, and hovers over me. He stares into my eyes, and he kisses me. He kisses me deeply.

I moan into his mouth. I drip between my thighs. I quiver with need beneath him.

God, I've missed his kiss.

He pulls back and stares into my eyes again, and we're both panting. "Lift your arms," he says roughly. I do, and he pulls my t-shirt over my head. "Fuck, no bra," he says, and grabs my breasts in his hands, fondling and squeezing them. Then he starts giving my breasts amble attention with his mouth and his tongue.

My inner vixen is panting and moaning and gripping her sheets as I give her visual after visual of Carter indulging in me.

He kisses my breasts, wet, succulent kisses. He licks my nipples, flicking his tongue back and forth. And he takes my nipples into his mouth, sucking each one hard.

I'm moaning and panting simultaneously. I'm dripping and dripping, filling my thong with my arousal.

God, I've missed his mouth and his tongue.

I arch my back a little and feed him more of my breasts, and at the same time, I try and maneuver my thong off of me.

He releases my breasts and stares into my eyes. "Let me help you," he says, and then he grips my thong in his hand and rips it off my pussy with one powerful yank.

I gasp, my mouth open, and he grins at me, sexy, hungry, and mischievously.

God, that was so hot.

"I've missed your taste," he says as he runs his thumb over my bottom lip. Then he kisses me. He kisses me with fiery lips and a fiery tongue.

But he quickly moves down my body, leaving my lips hot, until his face is hovering over my sex. He licks through my folds, and then he looks up at me. "I've missed your taste," he repeats, then licks through my folds again.

"Oh, Carter," I breathe between my continuous moaning and panting. I place my hands in his hair and watch him as he indulges in my taste.

His tongue licks through my folds. His mouth sucks on my entire pussy. He drinks my arousal with each lick and suck. And I grip his hair as small quivers vibrate through me.

Goddamn, I've really missed his mouth and his tongue.

Carter begins moaning all over my sex, licking and sucking and moaning. He grips my thighs, spreading me open wider, and he devours me more intensely.

"Oh, Carter," I breathe between my louder moans and heavier panting.

"My sexy Savannah, my sweet pussy," he murmurs on my glistening wet folds.

Oh god! I fist his hair in my hands, throw my head back, arching off the bed, and I come in his mouth, my thighs shaking in his hands.

"Carter! Oh, Carter," I exclaim.

But he doesn't stop. He keeps going, licking and sucking and moaning and holding me open for him.

My orgasm dissipates, leaving my whole body to tingle, but with each lick and suck, my body starts building toward another great climax.

Four days without him, without my Carter, and my entire body is screaming his name. Every single inch and piece of me has missed him.

"Mine," he growls on my soaking wet folds.

Oh shit!

His vocals vibrate through my folds and against my swollen clit, and then through the rest of my body.

"Carter!" I shout, and move my hands to the sheets, clawing at them as I come in his mouth once again. "Oh, Carter, oh Carter," I exclaim, writhing on the bed and shaking in his hands.

He licks and swallows everything I spill out, everything I give him. Then he looks up at me and licks his lips. "I'm so hard for you," he says, then moves up my body, his cock leaking a great deal of pre-cum between my thighs.

"You're dripping. Let me taste," I say, my voice breathy.

He catches a nice amount of his arousal between his forefinger and thumb, and then he brings his sticky seepage to my mouth, where I open up and suck his taste onto my tongue.

"Mm, yum," I voice, and lick my lips.

"You are so sexy," he says, positioning the head of his cock at my wet entrance.

"And all yours," I add, pushing my sex around his tip.

"You are so perfect, and I am so lucky." He drops his mouth to mine, kissing me with adoration, and his cock twitches inside my very wet opening.

"Carter," I breathe on his lips.

He pushes his cock the rest of the way inside me, filling me with his thickness, his hardness, his length. And I wrap myself around him as he thrusts with slow but infusing strokes, making unhurried, beautiful love to me.

His cock pushes slowly in. His cock pulls slowly out. Over and over, our bodies crushed together in love. It feels so good.

God, I've missed his cock, so much.

My body is singing his praises, singing his name, as I tingle all over, from my head to my toes. I feel so good.

His body is humming against mine, humming inside me, as he fills me with his burning heat. He feels so good.

"I've missed you," he murmurs on my lips. "I've missed this." He thrusts slowly in. "I can't go this long without you again." He pulls slowly out.

"I'm not going anywhere," I breathe on his lips.

He pushes slowly inside me and throbs hard against my swelling walls.

God, I've missed him. I've missed him so much.

He moves his mouth to my ear. "I love you," he whispers in it. Then he moves his mouth to my other ear. "So much," he whispers in it. And then I quiver in his arms.

He brings his lips back to mine and kisses me with the same adoration all over again.

And I come. And my orgasm provokes his orgasm, and he comes, too.

I shake in his arms and release a river of sweet fluids all around his cock, in-between our bodies, and onto the cotton sheets beneath me, continuously moaning into his mouth.

He throbs inside my inner wall's grip, continuously moaning into my mouth as well.

And he doesn't stop his slow thrusts or his filling me deep. He still gives me stroke after stroke.

His cock pushes slowly in. His cock pulls slowly out. Over and over, my walls continue to squeeze him.

"I want to stay buried inside you all night," he murmurs on my lips, making so much more unhurried, beautiful love to me.

"I'm all yours," I breathe on his lips, and he deepens our kiss even more.

And he takes me to ecstasy, loving me like no one else ever has, and like no one else ever will.

Chapter Eighteen

"It's us," I observe, smiling at the fairly big painting that Carter just placed in my hands.

He comes up behind me and circles his arms around me. "It is," he murmurs next to my ear.

"God, it's so erotic. I can feel the lust. I can hear the moans. It's so hot."

Carter has painted the two of us in the complete throes of passion. I'm positioned in his lap, his cock disappearing inside me. He's on his bent knees, somewhat sitting back on his heels with his arms wrapped around me. My legs are straddled around him, and my toes are pushing off the bed as I'm arching back with my head thrown back, one arm stretched out from me with my palm flat on the bed and balancing me, my other arm hanging on around his neck, my eyes closed, and my mouth open. He's off his heels a little as he's leaning into me and sucking on my nipple. The bed is all white, and the background is all orange, yellow, and red flames. He's captured our red-hot love and our intense heat, and he's captured all of it flawlessly.

"You're not only my muse," he murmurs next to my ear, "but you are also my leading lady. I love painting you." He kisses my neck.

"You must be in love," I tease, smiling, and I set the painting down on his bed.

"Deeply and totally in love with you in every way," he murmurs on my neck, and kisses me there. "You dominate my creativity, my dreams, and all my waking thoughts."

I turn in his arms, and then move my hands up his abs, his chest, and around his neck. "Ditto," I agree, and kiss his lips.

He moves his hands down to my backside and squeezes my ass cheeks as he slips his tongue in my mouth and makes me moan.

But I pull back before I moan again. "We have to go," I tell him, although I'd like nothing more than to stay in his arms and have his mouth and tongue all over me.

"I know," he says, then kisses my lips softly. "Let's go." He releases me, but grabs my hand, entwining our fingers. "I'll sneak you away later," he says, and it's a promise.

It is yet again another Friday night, another night at Intoxication, and another night of my sensual and erotic words. Carter manages to sneak me away just about every Friday night now, between my performances, and I love it. It fuels my sin and sexy even more.

"I'm counting on it," I say, and kiss his cheek.

He escorts me out of his loft and onto the street, where he hails us a cab. Then we're on our way to Chicago's coolest bar.

*　　　*　　　*　　　*　　　*　　　*　　　*　　　*

"You're looking at me like you want to eat me," I say to Carter as we're sitting at the bar.

"I do, and I will," he responds, his eyes growing darker and roaming all over my body.

I'm dressed in a backless halter neck plunged dress. It has quite revealing slits on each side, completely exposing my thighs, and it falls a couple inches above my knees. It's all a blackish-gray color, basically just covering my ass, my pussy, and my tits, although it shows much cleavage. It's very sinfully sexy. I have black and silver high heel stilettos with silver sandal bling on my feet, and they're very sexy. My fingernails and my toenails are painted red, and so are my lips. My eyelashes are heavy in black mascara, and my hair is up in a neat ponytail. I feel like a sexy vixen, ready to sin. And from the looks that I'm getting from Carter, he's ready to commit some sin.

But he looks tempting, too. He's dressed in gray jeans, a red cotton paristyle shirt with gray on the inside of the collar, gray on the inside where it buttons all the way down, gray on the outside of the pocket, and the cuffs are also gray when folded, which they are. It's a very sexy collar button-down dress shirt. He's got the top two buttons undone, and I kind of want to rip the rest of it open, maybe later tonight. His feet are covered in black matte dress shoes, and he has sexy stubble on his face, which I want to scratch my fingers in when we kiss, and I will at some point of the evening.

I'm about to react to his statement, but the MC takes the stage, interrupting my thoughts and my comeback.

"Ladies and gentlemen," he begins, "it's time to feel the sultry music. It's time to hear the erotic words. It's time to be seduced by our next performer, and if you're the lucky ones, you'll get a sexy drawing to take home." The crowd enthusiastically whistles and loudly claps. "Please welcome the exquisite, Savannah Lewis, and her favorite artist, Carter Bennett."

The crowd shows us their love and excitement with their hoots, hollers, whistles, and claps. They're full of energy and very noisy. It's a good, welcoming feeling.

Carter gives me a chaste kiss, even though I know he would rather give me a deep, dirty one, but I'm sure he will after this. And then he takes my hand, and we walk onto the stage.

For the past couple of weeks, Carter has become a part of my performance, an intriguing part. As the music is playing and I'm speaking my poetry, he's off to the side of me sketching a couple he's chosen from the crowd. The picture is always of the couple in a steamy, hot embrace of some kind, and everyone loves the new addition to Friday nights here, so do I.

I take the Mic, and Carter takes a seat near me, just a few feet back. He has an easel with a large, blank sketch paper in front of him. He picks up the black graphite pencil and looks out into the audience, scanning the couples. Then he whispers, "Ready, Gorgeous." And that's my cue.

I turn my head and nod at the band behind us, and they immediately begin to play a smooth, instrumental jazz piece. Carter begins to sketch, and I look out into the audience, ready to give them what they came for.

The music sinks into my pores and vibrates through my whole body as the piano sings and the drums beat. I start to slowly sway my hips to the rhythms, and the words flow out of me suggestively.

One Night

"Words are powerful. Touching is powerful. They are both covered in arousal, and then they take you and claim you, awakening powerful love."

A few loud whistles spread through the bar.

Slowly, sultry, and sensually, I begin.

Arouse me with your words.
Touch me with your determined, succulent kisses.
Take me to ecstasy.
Fill me with your creamy wishes.
Love all over me and deep inside.
I'm your girl.
And from you, I'll never hide."

More whistles fill the bar, loud and shrill.

I turn my head and look at Carter. He looks up and locks eyes with me, grinning invitingly, just for me. I wink and blow him a kiss, and then I turn back and face my fans again.

"He opened me everywhere with his words, his touch, and his kisses, and he awakened my love."

"I love you, Savannah!" an older gentleman in the crowd shouts.

"And so do I," Carter whispers, for only me to hear.

I smile, from my fans, but more importantly from my man. Then my name is chanted by everyone, but only for a minute, and then a hush falls on the bar.

Slowly, sultry, and sensually, I continue, the music continuously putting me in a sensuous zone.

"Awakening Love
The air is thick
Seducing us with desire
Pulling us close
Closer
Crushing our bodies together
A deep need that's taking over
Awakening Love
So I climb onto his lap

And take him in my wet opening
He pulsates inside me
As I ride him up and down
I grip his hair
He grips my backside
Our bodies glued together as one
Awakening love
We're indulging ferociously
Awakening love
With swollen lips
From his hard, lustful kiss
With electrified skin
From his rousing touches
My heated core
From his fierce eyes
His body gives me life
Awakening Love"

Carter puts down his pencil and stands up, showing the crowd his sketch. It's a couple in one another's arms with them both pressing a hand to the other's heart as they stare into each other's eyes. It's beautiful and sexy.

My fans, the entire bar, clap and cheer loudly and begin rising to their feet. I hear my name mixed in with their whistles, hoots, and hollers. And I give them an ear to ear smile.

Carter jumps off the stage and gives the drawing to the lucky couple, and they're ecstatic, thanking him with huge smiles and hugs. And I don't blame them, because Carter is so amazing, and he is so, so talented.

"Thank you," I tell the crowd. I blow them a kiss, and then I leave the stage, joining my man.

The music changes to an upbeat rock and roll rhythm, and Carter wastes no time. He quickly takes my hand and leads me away, away to our favorite unoccupied office.

The room instantly fills with heat as Carter locks the door and advances toward me with hungry eyes, making me paralyzed by his eagerness. I bite my bottom lip, my breathing already quickening as I anticipate his touch and his kiss.

He grabs my backside in both of his hands, gripping it firmly and squeezing it repeatedly, making my breathing louder, my insides hot, and my sex to dampen with my arousal. He brings his mouth to mine and says against my lips, "Keep your hands on the desk." He kisses me hard, but then stops. "Do it now," he says.

I grab the edge of the desk behind me, and Carter crushes my lips, kissing me hard and vehemently. I moan and moan into his mouth and leak and leak into my thong, and then he releases me everywhere and drops to his knees in front of me, leaving my lips a bit swollen and my chest rising and falling quickly from my panting.

Damn!

"I love this dress," he says, freeing my breasts. "You're so accessible," he says, moving my thong to the side. "Spread your legs," he tells me, and I do.

He grips my thighs and dives right in, burying his face in my pussy, licking and sucking like he's dying of thirst, like he's starving, and enjoying it like it's his last meal.

I grip the desk harder, watching him devour me, watching him coax my pleasure, watching him coax my orgasm. And I moan and moan, and pant and pant, leaning my backside into the desk.

He lets his hands trail all over my body, then he moves two fingers to my wetness, sticks them inside but pulls them right back out. And then he makes me moan so fucking loud as he slowly pushes those two fingers into my anus. He starts pushing them in and out, and I'm stuck in-between his face and his fingers, being turned out and feeling deliciously debauched.

Goddamn, the pressure feels so good.

He glides his available fingers over my breasts, over my nipples, around my breasts, underneath my breasts, and along the sensitive sides of them, one breast and the other, back and forth and back and forth, making my nipples harden.

He tugs on my nipples hard. He licks and sucks my pussy fiercely. He pushes two fingers in and out of my anus a little faster. He's committed to my pleasure and to my orgasm. He's determined to take them both, and I'm ready to give him what he wants and satisfy us both.

"Oh, Carter," I breathe, "Carter." Huge waves of pleasure wash over me, and I'm drowning in orgasmic bliss.

He begins growling on my sex, and I begin humping against his face and throwing my ass onto his fingers. I'm just so close, and then I'm there.

"Oh... Oh... Oh... Oh... Shit!" I come hard, so fucking hard and explode in his mouth.

I throw my head back, my fingernails scratching the desk in my grip, my body quivering in small shocks as I ride out ripple after ripple of my extreme orgasm.

I'm completely overcome by Carter's ability and technique. If he didn't have me locked in his aggressive clenches, I'd be falling back on the desk or falling to the floor.

Carter slowly withdraws his fingers, and then slowly pulls his face off me as I slowly come down from my high.

He stands up, grips my backside, and kisses me. "We'll continue this later in bed," he says on my lips, then kisses me again and keeps kissing me.

"Mm, with lube and a dildo," I murmur against his lips, and he squeezes my ass cheeks.

"And my dick," he says against my lips, and squeezes my cheeks again.

"So dirty," I breathe into his mouth.

"Filling your pussy and your ass simultaneously, very dirty," he says, then kisses me once more, and then releases me.

Damn, I cannot wait for this night to end, even though I love my fans and I love what I do.

I put my breasts back in my dress and fix my thong, but I'm in need of a thorough cleaning. "I need the bathroom before we go back out there." Tissues won't be enough. I need paper towels, and I need to wet a couple to clean myself up.

"Let's go, Gorgeous." He takes my hand, and we leave the office and go straight to the bathrooms, where we each enter in the designated doors.

I clean myself and dry myself and my thong, check my reflection in the mirror, and then I exit, and Carter is finished as well and waiting for me. Then we walk, hand in hand, to the bar.

Steve gives us a knowing smile as we take a seat on the barstools, and then he places a shot of whiskey in front of me and one in front of Carter.

We swallow back our shots, and Abby sips on her mixed drink, Purple Haze, as she sits next to me.

"That drawing was beautiful, Carter," Abby says.

"Thank you." He smiles.

Just then, a woman approaches me, but she's not super energized or carrying one of my books, like a fan of mine would be. She is smiling very brightly though, so I smile back.

"Savannah Lewis," she says. "I'm Jamie Stone, from 103.5 KISS FM." She extends her hand to me.

Wow, she's from one of the local radio stations, a top 40 radio station that serves all of Chicago. "Hi, it's nice to meet you," I say, rising off my stool and shaking her hand.

"Likewise," she says. She turns her attention briefly to Carter and Abby and introduces herself, and then she turns all of her attention back to me.

She knows who I am, which is so cool, because I listen to that radio station, among a few others.

"I'm starting a new radio show. It will be at night, from eight to midnight, Monday through Thursday, and I would like you to be a part of it," Jamie tells me. "It's a show that will discuss sex and relationships. I've read some of your work, and I've seen you perform, and I think you would be a great asset, plus you have a great voice and great sex appeal that shines through when you speak."

I'm overjoyed by her offer and her compliments. I don't even think twice before opening my mouth. "That sounds really fun and something that I would like to be a part of."

"Excellent. I'm glad to hear that." She reaches in her pristine jeans pocket and pulls out a business card, handing it to me. "Give me a call on Monday, and we can further discuss all the details."

"Thank you. I will." I smile from ear to ear.

"You're a rising star, Savannah," she confidently says. "I'm going to stick around for your next performance. Your words engross me, just like everyone else here tonight."

"You're kind, thank you."

"You're a natural," she says. "You glow up there." And she disappears back into the crowd.

"I'm so happy for you," Abby says, smiling, as I sit back down between her and Carter.

"I'm so proud of you," Carter says, "and I'm even more proud to have you on my arm and to be able to call you mine." He kisses my cheek. "She's right, you're a rising star."

"Thank you." I kiss his lips softly.

"I'm going to have a famous best friend," Abby excitedly says, bouncing a little on her stool. "Just don't forget about me."

"Never," I tell her with a big smile.

And then our conversation gets interrupted by a swarm of my fans, all grinning from ear to ear and each carrying one or more than one of my books.

I rise off my stool again and greet them. I chat with them for a while, all of us having a fun conversation. They all gush their praises and appreciation for my work, which makes me feel amazing. It always does. Then I sign each and every book, and I take pictures with them, too. They all happily merge back into the crowd, and then the MC takes the stage.

"Ladies and gentlemen," the MC begins, "please welcome back the amazing duo, Miss Savannah Lewis and Mr. Carter Bennett." The audience whistles, cheers, and claps, and it's all very loud, which fills me with adrenaline each and every time.

I love what I do!

Carter takes my hand, and we walk onto the stage. He takes a seat at his easel, picking up his black graphite pencil, and I grab the Mic. He looks out to the audience and scans the couples, and then he whispers, "Ready, Gorgeous."

I nod at the band behind us, and they begin playing their instruments. Smooth jazz fills my ears and spreads through my whole body, and I start swaying my hips to the sultry beats. I look out to my fans and begin, speaking in a slow and sexy tone.

"A kiss... A kiss is to touch with the lips. It's a sign of sexual desire. It's a sign of love."

A few loud whistles disperse through the bar.

"He touches me with his lips, loving me as if there's someone working every hour, every minute of the day to take me from him."

A few more whistles bounce off the walls.

"But I can't be taken from him, because he's marked me with true love's kiss."

The crowd gets loud with enthusiasm.

"I'm marked, too," Carter whispers, for only me to hear.

I smile out to my fans and wait for them to quiet down as my heart smiles from my man's words. Then I continue.

"Kiss me hard with your love
Lather me in passion
Wrap me in your warmth
Make me your obsession
Kiss me hard with your love
Fill me with blazing heat
I feel you in my core
You make my heart skip a beat
Kiss me hard with your love
Paint the canvas of my heart
With each dominating stroke
Filling me deep
Kiss me hard with your love
Thrusting on repeat
Throbbing and stilling
Pulling out and pushing back in
Kiss me hard with your love
Take me to ecstasy
Worship my body
It's your work of art
Kiss me hard with your love"

Carter puts down his pencil and stands up, showing the crowd his sketch. It's a couple kissing passionately as they are pressed against each other's naked flesh. It's beautiful. It's tasteful. It's so steamy.

And just like earlier, my fans, the entire bar, clap and cheer loudly and begin rising to their feet. I hear my name being chanted. I hear my favorite artist's name being chanted. I hear "amazing duo" being chanted. It's all mixed in with their whistles, hoots, and hollers. And I can't stop smiling.

Carter jumps off the stage and gives the drawing to the lucky couple. And like the lucky ones before them, they're ecstatic, thanking him with huge smiles and hugs.

"Thank you," I tell everyone, speaking into the Mic. I blow a kiss to the audience, my audience. Then I leave the stage and join Carter at his side.

"Dirty fun," he whispers in my ear.

"Yes, please." I nod, and then I bite my bottom lip, anticipating the feeling of both of my holes being filled at the same time and being filled fully.

He takes my hand, threading his fingers through, and we proceed to escape the bar without having anyone stop us.

A sizzling hot and dirty night is calling to us, and we can't get out of here fast enough.

Chapter Nineteen

"Pack your bag, Gorgeous," Carter tells me, setting his phone down on his bed and grabbing two backpacks out of his closet. "I'm whisking you away."

He's so spontaneous, one of the qualities that I absolutely love about him.

"Where are we going?" I excitedly ask.

"I'm not telling." He grins, thoroughly enjoying his secret.

"Okay, I can deal with that." I smile. His enthusiasm is contagious. "But can you at least tell me how long we'll be away, and what type of clothing will I need?"

"We will be gone in warm temperatures with the sun shining for five days, and I plan on keeping you naked for most of our stay." He steps to me, places his hands on my hips, and pulls me snug against him.

"Really," I say, wrapping my arms around his neck.

"Yes, most definitely," he says, staring into my eyes.

"So a couple of bikinis, a couple of dresses..." I pause as his lips descend to mine and his hands inch toward my backside.

"Perfect," he murmurs on my mouth, and then he squeezes my ass cheeks and kisses me.

And this kiss is juicy, very juicy, as we grip each other tight and taste each other's tongues.

But he releases me all too soon. I kind of wanted to get naked right now.

"The cab will be here in thirty minutes," he informs me.

Oh, now I'm super excited. We can get naked once we get there.

We each grab a backpack and begin filling them, taking only the essentials and minimal clothing.

Carter and I have been going strong together for six months now, and I basically live with him. Most of my belongings are here, but I still stay at my apartment every so often. But once the lease is up, everyone will be moving in with their men full-time. I already consider my home to be with Carter though, and so does he. In one another's vicinity, we are inseparable.

The cab arrives as scheduled, and we are more than ready to go. I don't know where we are going, but I can't wait.

Carter and I have been very busy these past few months, but it's been a really great busy. He's been painting and drawing and selling his artwork on a regular basis. His gallery is doing very well. And I've been having a lot of fun working at the radio station four nights a week and at the bar on Friday nights. I'm getting a lot of wonderful responses, and I'm accumulating an even larger audience and more fans. Plus, I've been writing every chance that I get, and I finished and published my first full-length novel. We're each making our dreams our reality.

We are both making a name for ourselves, not just in the city, but our names are spreading through the state as well. We are both on our way to big-time statuses. Busy but happy, and this mysterious vacation will be a nice break.

*   *   *   *   *   *   *   *

Carter and I are in Hawaii, walking hand in hand along the beach shore, near where our first kiss took place. The night sky is clear and promising. The stars are twinkling, and the moon is glowing, shining light on the waves. It's a warm and beautiful night, and it holds so much meaning for us.

We had a long flight, nonstop for about nine hours, but we had a nice and romantic dinner after we arrived, even though we arrived fairly late. And now paradise is whispering to us with every warm and gentle breeze that touches us.

Carter and I together, in love, in Hawaii, it's picture-perfect.

Suddenly, Carter stops us in the sand and takes both of my hands in his. He stares into my eyes and says, "You are my breath of fresh air. You are my sunshine. I love you, and I want to spend the rest of my life with you." He releases my hands, drops down to one knee, and pulls out a ring from his jeans pocket. "My Savannah," he says, looking up into my eyes, so much love radiating from his, "will you make me the happiest man in the universe and marry me?"

There's no second thought. There's no hesitation. I belong with him, and he belongs with me.

"Yes!" I exclaim, smiling from ear to ear.

He stands up, grinning, looking just as happy as I am, and slips the ring on my finger, and it's beautiful. It's a princess cut diamond, one carat that sparkles on a white gold band. It fits perfectly, and it's never coming off.

"I love you," he says again, wrapping his arms securely around my waist.

"I love you, too." I wrap my arms around his neck and get lost in his darkening sapphires.

He kisses me, breathing all of his love and affection that he has for me into my mouth, and I melt against him as the water washes over our bare feet.

My whole world is right, and with Carter in my forever, it will never be wrong.

*   *   *   *   *   *   *   *

"And why can't we just have breakfast in bed?" I ask Carter as we enter the hotel restaurant. "I was quite comfortable there."

As new fiancés, we loved each other between the sheets all night long. We quivered and moaned, and my ring sparkled and shined, glistening off the walls. It was orgasmic heaven. It was totally and utterly perfect.

And now I want him naked every chance that I can get, but he said he has something for me at breakfast, so here we are. But once we're done eating, I'm running back to our room and stripping my sundress off and starting his naked plan, my naked plan.

We have five days here, and the countdown begins today. And I'm sort of hoping that we can get sinfully sexy around all kinds of places on the island, not just in our room. And since Carter wants me naked as much as possible, and I want him naked as much as possible, then I don't see that being a problem.

I'm wild, and he's impulsive. And that leads to some naughty, steamy actions in some risqué scenarios. This get away is going to be hot, red-hot.

"You're going to love what's waiting for you," he says, grinning, and his eyes holding another secret.

The hostess leads us to our table, and I cannot believe my eyes. My family is here, my mom and dad, Lacy and Brian, and Abby and Steve. Carter's family is here, too, his mom and dad and Caleb and Ashley. They are all smiling at us and looking over-the-top excited.

I'm shocked, but I'm happy. I give everyone a hug, and it's really great to finally meet his parents in person.

"What are you all doing here?" I say, sitting down in the chair that Carter pulled out for me, smiling but slightly confused. And I know I'm the only one in the dark about this current situation.

"Your fiancé wanted all of us here," my mom says. "Now let me see that ring."

I begin showing my mom and everyone else my ring, my hand outstretched and moving slowly around the table.

"How do you all know about the proposal?" I ask.

"It's all part of my brother's plan," Caleb says, giving Carter a knowing look and smile.

Carter turns his head toward me. "I want to marry you today, tonight actually, on the beach."

"What?" I blurt out in surprise.

"Everything is all planned and ready," he tells me. "All you need to do is get a dress."

Wow! His spontaneity is surreal. I love it, and I don't want to wait either. I'm ready to be his for forever and ever.

"Yes." I smile at him. "I can't wait to marry you."

He kisses me, his lips lingering on mine for a minute or two, and I can sense everyone's approval and pleased hearts.

Then a waitress approaches our table and sets down big plates of food that consist of scrambled eggs, bacon, pancakes, assorted slices of melons, and assorted berries. We have mimosas to drink, and after everyone says their toasts and congratulations to us, we all begin consuming the delicious food. It's a wonderful breakfast, and now I'm glad that Carter made me get out of bed.

*   *   *   *   *   *   *   *

I've spent the entire day with my mom, Carter's mom, Lacy, Abby, and Ashley. We've be on the hunt for a dress for my wedding tonight, and I've found one. It's white. It's simple. It's beautiful.

Everyone's dressed and on the beach, and I'm waiting with my dad, unseen to everybody, waiting to become Mrs. Bennett.

My dress is long, flowing down to the ground, and the bodice is all lace with spaghetti straps. My hair is curled with half of it pinned up in a pearl clip and the other half of it spiraling down my back. My makeup is light, nothing too heavy, just black mascara and red lipstick. My feet are bare, and I hold a single long stem red rose in my hands. I'm so ready.

A soft guitar rhythm fills the air, and then I hear Caleb and Ashley quietly singing All You Need Is Love by The Beatles. My dad takes my hand and walks me into view. Everyone smiles at me, especially my man.

"You're gorgeous," Carter says, taking my hands.

"And you're very handsome," I tell him. He's dressed in all white, and his feet are bare.

The sun is setting, a reddish-orange color glowing in the sky as the sun slowly disappears over the midnight blue water. It's breathtaking to look at, but Carter's eyes are what have my full attention.

"Love is a powerful magic, captivating and fascinating," the officiant says. "And when you realize you want to spend the rest of your life with someone, you want to start the rest of your life as soon as possible."

His words couldn't be truer as Carter and I gaze into one another's eyes.

It's a quick, easy, laid-back wedding, but it's so very special.

"Savannah," Carter begins, "you've brightened my whole world, sparked a heat that's lit me up completely, inside and out, like a blazing inferno. I love the fire. I love you." He pauses for a few seconds, just staring into my eyes, and then continues. "I promise to always be free with you, to live in the moment with you, and to keep our flames burning hot." He slips a beautiful diamond encrusted ring on my finger, and it matches my engagement ring precisely.

And now it's my turn.

"Carter," I begin, "with every word you speak into my eyes, with every touch you glide across my body, with every kiss that tingles my lips, you bring me to life, and forever in your world is where I'll stay." I pause briefly, lost in his eyes, the only place that's worth being lost in, and then I continue. "I promise to always be your muse, inspiring you and loving you." I slide his ring off my flower stem and slip it on his finger. It's a diamond encrusted white gold band, and it looks great on him.

"I now pronounce you married," the officiant says.

Our family members whistle, cheer, and clap as Carter wraps his arms around me, dips me low, and kisses me hard, hard with love and hard with a promise for a sinfully sexy lifetime with him.

And my wild ass will make sure that promise is kept.

*   *   *   *   *   *   *   *

The air is warm and sultry on our skin. The sky is dark but filled with stars and a big moon. The night is young, and Carter has pulled me away from our small party.

"What would you like to do before I take you back to our room?" he asks me.

We're walking hand in hand in the secluded area where Carter and I first had some risqué fun, where we had our first kiss, and where he asked me to marry him. This beach will always hold extraordinary memories for us, and I want to make more, right here, right now.

"Let's go skinny dipping, but this time, let's do it for real, no underwear."

"Life's never going to be dull with you," he says, grinning and unbuttoning his shirt.

"Never," I agree, smiling and gradually wiggling out of my dress.

"I love you," he says, "my Savannah."

One Night

"I love you, my Carter."

He takes my hand, and we run, both of us fully naked, and we dash into the crashing waves.

He enfolds me in a delicious kiss, and I've finally found that piece of me that was left here.

And they live in an artistic, heated ever after...

One Night

Thank you for reading One Night, Carter and Savannah's spicy, red-hot love story. I hope that you will give this book a review on Amazon. Reviews really do help independent authors be found by new readers.

Visit my Amazon Author Page here:

http://amazon.com/author/eadeboest

Check out my Twitter account here:

http://twitter.com/EADeBoestauthor

Check out my Facebook account here:

http://facebook.com/eadeboest

Thank you again!

Acknowledgements

This book has been very exciting to write. I just listened to my characters and let their story unfold on the pages. I've had much encouragement that's kept the words flowing, even encouraging whispers from my characters. And I couldn't be happier with the passion and love that's been created.

I would like to thank my family. First, my husband, he makes it possible for me to produce sizzling love stories. He works hard. He loves hard. He holds it down. He's always willing to give me a listening ear, and he's always willing to lend me advice. He's the best.

Second, my kids, they are my biggest cheerleaders with their enthusiasm, their smiles, and their contagious energy. They are proud of their mommy, and that warms my heart.

Third, my friends, they are always understanding and always supportive. They are along for the ride and enjoying my journey.

And last, but certainly not least, my readers, I write these stories for you. I love it when I get your feedback, your messages, and your reviews. As long as you keep on loving my characters, I will continue to create new ones for you, always keeping it deliciously sexy and passionately hot.

Thank you!
XOXO
E. A. DeBoest

Books by E. A. DeBoest

Construction of the Heart Series

Construction of the Heart Vol 1
Sealing of the Heart Vol 2
Expansion of the Heart Vol 3

My first stand alone novel

One Night

And more to come!

I have many more character's stories to tell. So stay tuned, because I'm always busy and working hard, filling the pages with words that fill your body with heat.
Happy Reading XO

Made in the USA
Coppell, TX
04 January 2024

27278910R00103